About the Author

Born in Kilmarnock, Scotland but spent the majority of life growing up in the north east of England. Left school with very few qualifications, but eventually did gain a Master's Degree at Teesside University.

Married to Ann for thirty-seven years, with two grown up boys, Fergus and Ross.

A long and varied career to date that includes: Golf Professional, Electrician, Geologist working in Angola, Zaire, Gabon, Nigeria and the USA, Police Officer (Dog handler, operating general purpose German Shepherd dogs and specialist drugs dogs). After leaving the police force career continued as a Sales Person, General Manager, Operations Director, Commercial Director and Managing Director; now able to add published author to the list and not ready for retirement yet – the fun has only just begun.

Zeelandia and the Gateway Stone

.

H. A. Cowan

Zeelandia and the Gateway Stone

Olympia Publishers
London

.

www.olympiapublishers.com
OLYMPIA PAPERBACK EDITION

A CIP catalogue record for this title is
available from the British Library.

ISBN: 978-1-78830-448-1

This is a work of fiction.
Names, characters, places and incidents originate from the writer's
imagination. Any resemblance to actual persons, living or dead, is
purely coincidental.

First Published in 2019

Olympia Publishers
60 Cannon Street
London
EC4N 6NP
Printed in Great Britain

Dedication

I would like to dedicate this book to my long-suffering wife of thirty-seven years, Ann, without whose love and eternal support I would not have brought these characters to life, or had the courage to have this book published.

I would like to thank Ann, my son Fergus and my daughter-in-law Fiona, for their unwavering enthusiasm and critique of my work and for pushing me to make sure that this book was finished and that the further adventures of Zeelandia are captured for all to enjoy.

.

The Origins of The Gateway Stone

Good and evil have existed since before the origins of time itself. They survived without shape, form or substance, drifting many light years apart. There was no life, there was no meaning, and there was no purpose, yet in essence there were all of these things.

A cavalcade of meteors patrolled the night sky; they destroyed all in their way and engulfed the very essence of space and time with a choking dark blanket.

At the epicentre of darkness, a spirit ruled: Vandermortel, a champion of evil, whose malevolence knew no bounds.

A powerful sorcerer who used his skills well on a ceaseless journey, swallowing up all in his path, wreaking death and destruction to all who would stand in his way.

Space and time grew increasingly dark; Vandermortel grew ever stronger and charged on relentlessly through the vastness and eternity of space, sucking out the very essence of life wherever it could be found.33

A resounding echo pulsated across the night sky. *"My Mother Earth, come to me, come to me, you shall be mine, all mine, and when I have done with you, I shall be unstoppable;*

not even Zeelandia, the guardian of souls, shall be able to threaten my dominance."

Vandermortel, distracted by his own self-indulgence and premature self-edification for another job well done, failed to see Zeelandia and her army of souls approach.

Suddenly and without warning, the vastness of space erupted into a crescendo of light whose intensity illuminated the very soul of the universe.

Vandermortel was startled; his guard was down; who would dare to challenge his dominance over the universe?

The dark riders of the apocalypse, his escorts and protectors, reared up in defence of their lord and master, but their response was futile and ineffective. They were no match for the surge of power rained down upon them by Zeelandia.

Zeelandia summoned up all of her strength and directed a tirade of blows on her startled opponent. Vandermortel rose fiercely, his dark shape once again casting a sinister shadow over the entire universe; he was twisting and writhing, trying to escape Zeelandia's grasp, his misshapen body in torment, but it was to no avail.

Zeelandia's back was arched; she reared back and faced her opponent. In rhythmical motion, her arms outstretched, thousands upon thousands of pulsating beads of light erupted from her fingertips, each one directed with pinpoint accuracy at Vandermortel and his allies. First her right hand, then her left, again and again and again.

As the beads of light struck her foe, each one appeared to explode into a million smaller beads, more illuminating and intense than ever before, rendering all that they struck motionless and powerless to fight back.

As Zeelandia inhaled, Vandermortel was drawn ever closer to her; this time there was no escape. All around Zeelandia a breathtaking light show ensued; the souls of the universe had joined together to rid the universe of this evil, who for so long had cast a dark and menacing cloud over the perpetuity of space and time.

Vandermortel was drawn clear of his allies, many of whom, exposed and devoid of any direction, fled the scene like rats deserting a sinking ship; others, his closest and most devout followers, attempted one last time to break the spell Zeelandia had cast over him.

The bright lights exuded by the souls of the universe blinded both Vandermortel and those followers left by his side and rendered them powerless to fight back.

Small bright lights flickered ever brighter and danced in formation, perfectly choreographed. Zeelandia reached out her arm and touched the tortured soul that lay before her.

A spectacular noise resounded all around, and with one final synchronised movement the bright flickering lights devoured Vandermortel and imprisoned him in a casket made out of their own being. His dark soul was captured and imprisoned for all to see within the *"Gateway Stone"*.

Vandermortel's allies and protectors, those who were not quick enough to escape Zeelandia's onslaught, were imprisoned with Vandermortel; others were banished to walk blind though the universe for all of eternity.

Drained and weary after the battle, Zeelandia stopped on earth to rest and to decide what should be done with the Gateway Stone. She had been given no prior instruction by the council on what to do now. She was isolated and on her own.

Earth was not a pleasant place; it was dark, and silent — it sent a cold shiver through her tired body.

There was little substance to the landscape; hard volcanic rock rose from the earth's core as though drawn from great depths beneath the surface and pulled skyward by some gigantic mystical force.

Deep gorges, sucked clean and devoid of any moisture, meandered down the hillside and far out of sight. A thick cloud of stagnant grey dust enveloped the whole landscape and smothered everything in its path.

There was a silent, eerie atmosphere, no sign of life in any form; Vandermortel had done a good job here. Fortunately, his demise had come just in time to prevent Earth's total destruction, and although it would take several lifetimes to resurrect, this planet could and would recover and once again spawn new life.

Exhausted, Zeelandia fell into a deep sleep and immediately began to dream of a world where people could live in harmony with one another. One where love, trust and compassion formed the basis of a civilisation, where good ruled over evil and where the souls of the universe could find a resting place to watch over them for all eternity.

When Zeelandia awoke, the land before her was rich and green; tall trees shimmered in the light wind, their leaves rustling softly as the breeze caressed each and every one of them.

Beyond, a gentle river meandered slowly down the hillside, its waters crystal clear, transforming moments later into a crescendo of noise, as a waterfall altered its very being and created a dancing dragon, writhing and unstoppable; full of passion and character as it crashed into a deep blue pool below far below; emerging a few seconds later tamed, calm and at peace with its surroundings.

Zeelandia stood there, motionless, transfixed by the beauty surrounding her. Suddenly, she remembered her battle with Vandermortel. Where was the Gateway Stone? What had she done with it?

She looked ahead; a small figure appeared, slowly winding through the lush green fields in the distance. The fields were covered in a thick blanket of rich yellow buttercups. Small white daisies, clumped together, broke through the sea of yellow and brought focus and perspective to the landscape.

Butterflies danced as though in ecstasy and moved to the sound of some mystical tune played only for them.

As the outline drew nearer, Zeelandia could make out a tall, upright figure dressed in a long silver cloak. His face was covered, but from underneath the tightly fitting hood Zeelandia could see a long white beard. Small rimmed glasses adorned his face, which was heavily marked by the passing of time, and in itself told many stories of years gone by and of battles won and lost.

"Kingston, is it really you? Where have you come from? What is going on? Where is the Gateway Stone? And what of Vandermortel?"

"One thing at a time, my darling Zeelandia. There are many things we must speak of, but all in good time; we are reunited for now, but we must make the most of our time together, for I fear it will be far shorter than either of us can imagine." Zeelandia threw her arms round her uncle and hugged him tightly; she had never been so pleased to see anyone in her life.

The pair sat down under the shade of a large oak tree. Zeelandia listened intently as her uncle updated her on the events following her battle with Vandermortel.

"The souls of the universe continue to imprison Vandermortel and hold him captive within the Gateway Stone. The stone has been held within the vaults of Arcadia, protected by the guardians of the stone, by those and only those who could resist the temptation of looking at it."

"But why should…" Kingston pre-empted Zeelandia's next question. *"Anyone who dares to look at the stone and sees Vandermortel face to face runs the risk of being drawn to the dark side and shall become a slave to him for ever.*

"You have slept for many decades, my child; the battle you fought was hard and took its toll on you. More than even you may realise at present. During your long sleep the universe has been able to recover, and that which was once bleak and dark breeds new life, thanks to you."

Zeelandia sensed something uncomfortable in her uncle's voice. *"What's wrong, all that you have said so far, is it not good news, is there something else that your heart wishes to share but you are frightened to speak of?"*

"Your intuition is as good as ever, Zeelandia, and it is with a heavy heart that I must be the bearer of this sad news.

"One of the stone's guardians has been drawn to the dark side and has stolen the stone. He is at present unsure of his purpose, but Vandermortel is, as we speak, summoning up the dark riders of the apocalypse to track him down and take control over the stone."

"Is Vandermortel once again free?"

"No, Zeelandia, he remains a prisoner of the stone; the only way he can be set free is for the stone to be taken far away from Arcadia to the Mountains of Dean.

"There is one place, deep within the mountain range, a sacred mountain by the name of Mount Fleming, where the stone must be laid to rest. From this point the stone is exposed to the outside of the mountain on each of the north, south, east and west sides. If Vandermortel can conjure up the four Storms of Destiny and in unison their lightning strikes the stone, then the heat will be so intense that the unity of the souls of the universe will be broken and the stone will be no longer, and Vandermortel will be free.

"Members of the council wish to meet with you; we must do all in our power to prevent this from happening, but alas, we once again need to call on you for help."

The Summoning of Zeelandia

The powers of darkness grew stronger day by day. The world was changing, and not for the better. The guardians of the Gateway Stone were fully aware of their duty and what had to be done if they were to restore the balance of power.

Every day that passed, the world grew darker and the council knew that they had to act quickly if they were to succeed in their quest. If they could not succeed in preventing Vandermortel conjuring up his escape, then one of the universe's most powerful sorcerers would be free and the universe would once again be in mortal danger.

The large oval table ingrained with rich carvings, which depicted in minute detail the tapestry of all life within the universe, engulfed the stark hexagonally shaped chamber.

The walls appeared to be devoid of any colour or depth; there was no obvious source of light, or windows, yet the room was illuminated to such a degree that any mortal man would have been blinded by its irascible nature and lustre.

Zeelandia and Kingston sat patiently, taking up two seats adjacent to each other around the table. It brought back distant memories for Zeelandia; the preceding time she was summoned to the chamber was to prepare for her first, last and to date only battle with Vandermortel.

The dread and trepidation felt that day seemed to pale into insignificance compared to the feelings that were flowing uncontrollably through her body now.

She glanced momentarily in Kingston's direction, reaching out a hand towards him. Kingston gratefully accepted the gesture; deep down he was feeling every bit as unsettled as Zeelandia. Kingston knew what would be asked of Zeelandia; in reality, so did Zeelandia.

The chamber door opened, and through a mist of opaque crystal three figures entered the room; the door closed immediately behind them.

The two male figures and one female figure each took up their allotted places at the table. Initially all three were silent, but Zeelandia could tell from their expressions that all was not well in the land of Arcadia, and that more bad news was to follow.

The first to speak was Inchinnan, the head of the council, a man of slight build and sombre appearance. His face was elongated and gaunt, and like Kingston, he had a long white beard. His left eye was the most compelling shade of iridescent blue imaginable, but his right eye was as white as his facial hair and lifeless, the result of a tragic accident many years previously.

"Zeelandia, my child, Kingston I am sure has spoken with you regarding the theft of the Gateway Stone and the consequences we will all face if Vandermortel were to be set free."

"Yes, he has, Inchinnan, but what do you seek of me?"

"It is unfair of us to expect you to awake from your deep sleep and once again face the dangers posed by the dark side, but you, and you alone, have a heart pure enough to withstand the calling of Vandermortel, and the powers passed on to you by our guardians, although they may not be enough this time, make you our only hope of preventing Vandermortel being set free."

"But surely any of the guardians of the Gateway Stone are capable of this — they all have pure hearts."

"No, I am afraid not. One has already been drawn to the dark side, Lazonby. He was one of our most trusted guardians, one who has served us for many years, but alas, the temptation was too great, even for him, and he was pulled by Vandermortel's calling and looked into the stone."

"What of these dark riders of the apocalypse, where have they come from, and how will they know how to find the stone?"

"Alas, Zeelandia, the dark riders already have possession of the stone and make their way to Mount Fleming as we speak."

At that moment one of the remaining two council members arose from her chair and approached a section of the wall surrounding the room.

Her name was Ballantine, a lady of stout, upright appearance. Her hair was as gold as gold itself and her eyes bright and awake.

Her face was smooth and gave no hint as to what could be construed as age. A robe adorned her body from head to toe – each fibre could clearly be seen, each one a slightly different shade of silver.

Ballantine gently raised the bottom of her robe above her knees and quietly knelt before the wall. She raised her hands far above her head and began to recite some form of rhyme which neither Zeelandia nor Kingston could fully understand.

"Amatay, saroo formantle, comosay, revastle celtamori."

Although the words to start with in themselves could not be fully understood, both Zeelandia and Kingston knew, however, that the dialect was that of ancient Arcadian, a language spoken by the first guardians of Arcadia many thousands of years ago, a language powerful in meaning, and used only in the past by influential sorcerers who ruled Arcadia to fight against the powers of evil for the good of the universe.

Zeelandia listened intently; suddenly, the words took on a new meaning, inexplicably, and somehow, she was able to understand the significance of each of the words recited.

She was confused, unaware of what was happening; how could she understand the powerful words used by Ballantine? Only those serving as council members and the great White Queens of ancient transcript understood the dialect or could use the full power of the dialect to influence matters that until now, she had little knowledge of.

Ballantine again recited the words in a very quiet manner. *"Amatay, saroo formantle, comosay, revastle celtamori."*

Slowly, the whole wall changed from pure white to a translucent rainbow of colours with no apparent focal point. Then, almost instantaneously, it changed once again into a sharply focused picture.

The hillside was steep; tall trees stood upright at acute angles to the lush vegetation, which covered the ground.

Midway up the slope a small dark opening could barely be seen.

A thick fog enveloped the opening as though realising it was under surveillance, and immediately tried to hide this place from prying eyes, but it was too late.

The focus moved away from the landscape and began to cut through the thick fog to reveal a hidden area beyond.

Bridgewater, the third member of the council, who appearance-wise appeared almost as a clone of Inchinnan, not quite as gaunt, but equally sombre, arose from his seat to explain what was happening.

When walking he relied heavily upon a walking stick the like of which Zeelandia had never seen before. Every time Zeelandia glanced at the walking stick, it appeared to change colour ever so slightly, and she would swear, if asked, that it was pulsating in time with her own heartbeat.

Zeelandia was also convinced that the stick was spending as much time assessing her as she was it; and could it possibly be watching her every move through the single deep red ruby that adorned a silver-coloured handle at its very tip?

Bridgewater spoke very softly as though not wishing to give away their position to those on the other side of the screen.

"Ballantine has taken us to where the stone presently lies with Lazonby. Not all that we will witness shall be pleasant; unfortunately, we are to witness Lazonby's demise. However, through his heart and soul we will be able to journey with the stone, through the four Kingdoms of Destiny, and if Vandermortel is successful, to a resting place inside Mount Fleming.

Lazonby could barely be seen; his hunched figure was crouched next to a dark, damp wall to one side of the cave, which was almost in complete darkness.

He was trembling from head to toe and was muttering some kind of gibberish, which made no sense at all; he was clearly terrified.

Beside him, lying on the ground and covered by a black cloak, lay a spherical object about the size of a large melon.

The cloak was pulsating infrequently, and each time it did so a very low frequency tone was emitted and appeared to reverberate around the chasm for an eternity, as though searching for some hidden force to seek it out and capture it.

From some distance away, a faint sound could be heard. Lazonby appeared to become more and more agitated. Within the blink of an eye the faint sound took on a more sinister form.

The rhythmical beats grew louder and louder; the ground began to vibrate and shudder in time with the beats. The cave, which appeared dark, grew even darker, the noise became almost unbearable and then almost as suddenly as it began, the noise faded and the cave became silent once more.

Zeelandia knew deep down what was happening: the dark riders of the apocalypse were approaching the cave and there was nothing any of them could do but watch in dismay.

Each of them urged Lazonby to make some kind of retreat, to remember that he was still a guardian of the stone and to try to make good his escape.

For all that they wished, they knew deep in their hearts it could not be, as once Vandermortel has you within his grasp, it is futile to resist the calling of the dark side, and your soul is his to do with as he pleases.

An eerie silence fell over the cave. Outside tens of thousands of dark riders guarded its entrance. The stone began to emit a pulsating resonance more frequently than before. Although no identifiable sound could be heard, you could feel the pulses as they transcended back and forth across the cave, bouncing off one wall, then another.

Lazonby slowly removed the cloak, which adorned the Gateway Stone, and the dark, damp cave immediately took on a new, more sinister form.

Where there was only darkness, the light emitted from the stone searched out every crevice within the cave. Small, dark shapes could be seen fleeing from the light and hiding under rocks wherever they could be found. These small creatures were panwas, similar in size and shape to rats, but carrying enough venom in one small bite to incapacitate a fully-grown man within seconds.

Lazonby appeared paralysed by fear; he was unable to move and unable to talk. A dark shadow cast itself over the entrance to the cave. A tall, stark figure more than three metres in height filled the entire opening. Dressed in a black cloak, the upright figure was both menacing and imposing.

Hanging from a sheath around his waist, a long silver blade could be seen; in his left hand the outline of a ruby-incrusted dagger was just about visible.

This was Solway, previously Vandermortel's right-hand man and leader of the dark riders of the apocalypse.

When Vandermortel was captured, Solway had been sent far away from the battle to prepare for the day he would be needed to help his master escape.

Vandermortel trusted Solway implicitly; Solway had followed his instructions without question and had spent many decades preparing for this day, deep in space.

In hearing the call from his master, Solway was only too happy to answer.

Solway moved with lightning speed and plunged his dagger deep into Lazonby's chest. He slowly removed a black leather glove from his right hand, exposing his long-pointed fingers with sharp spear-like nails adorning the ends.

Lazonby was lying on the ground, mortally wounded, staring directly into the cold, motionless eyes of Solway.

Solway knelt beside him and without warning thrust his hand deep inside the open wound, twisted his wrist round, and with one single motion pulled Lazonby's still beating heart from his chest.

Solway then placed the heart into an opaque liquid, contained within a tall-lidded glass container.

Zeelandia heard herself scream out and immediately turned towards Kingston, burying her head deep into his chest; she began to sob uncontrollably.

A few minutes later, she raised her head and asked why so cruelly Solway had taken Lazonby's heart.

Bridgewater explained that without the heart of a guardian, Vandermortel could not be freed. Not only did the Gateway Stone have to be struck by the lightning of four storms simultaneously; a pure heart had to be sacrificed to the masters of the dark side.

When both are struck by lightning, the flames will intensify and the stone shall be no more, and Vandermortel will once again be free.

Solway placed the container holding Lazonby's heart inside his long cloak; he then turned to the Gateway Stone and picked it up gently, caressing it with both hands.

He looked deep into the epicentre of the stone; Vandermortel could be clearly seen sitting on a black horse with dark riders on either side of him.

Vandermortel spoke in a low, resounding tone. *"You have done well, my friend Solway; when I am free, you shall be well rewarded. We must, however, make haste to Mount Fleming; we have but one chance in every hundred years for this opportunity. The journey will not be an easy one, the path ahead treacherous, but the rewards far greater than you can ever imagine."*

Solway made no reply to his master. He turned around quickly and silently, his long cape swirling round as he changed direction.

Solway would be happy to spend an eternity in torture rather than not serve his master, a fact that had not gone unnoticed by Vandermortel, and this was the reason Vandermortel had chosen Solway as his one and only opportunity for freedom.

Solway walked towards the cave's exit, he took one step outside and held the Gateway Stone high above his head.

As far as the eye could see, thousands upon thousands of dark riders of the apocalypse spread out along the valley below.

In one synchronised movement they dismounted from their horses and simultaneously and without instruction knelt before their lord and master.

Zeelandia, still shaking from the events she had just witnessed, turned to Bridgewater. *"Now that the dark riders* have Vandermortel back, how can we stop them from doing what is necessary to set him free?"

Bridgewater went on to explain that the complete journey could be witnessed from where they sat and outlined the treachery of a journey which would see Vandermortel and his allies attempting to transcend four dangerous lands before they would finally reach Mount Fleming.

The council were mindful of the fact that this day may come and had in advance called upon the lords of the four Kingdoms of Destiny to seek out their support, should it be needed.

Unfortunately, it was with a sad and heavy heart that the council now needed to hastily arrange a meeting of the four lords and their advisers to determine the exact path of resistance that would be put up, and what help, support and resources would be needed for the battles ahead.

Bridgewater stood up. "*We have but seven days to put into action our preparation for the battles ahead, to engage with our allies and agree our strategy. We must be ready to do battle in each of the four kingdoms and eventually if required, within Mount Fleming.*"

Zeelandia, although unsure as to how she could contribute, knew deep in her heart that the council expected something of her, or she would not be there.

Inchinnan spoke once again: "*Zeelandia, I am sure you are still not fully aware of your powers. You fought a brave and dangerous battle to defeat Vandermortel before. Your powers were great then, but to succeed in this battle you will need to fully understand and embrace all that you are capable of.*

"We have arranged for you to visit a very sacred place, a land that does not in reality even exist, one which is written about in the sacred scriptures and a land that can only be accessed once in all eternity for the good of the universe."

Zeelandia knew exactly what Inchinnan spoke of; as a small girl she was told that her mother was one so special that she was taken to this place, leaving Zeelandia and her father behind. Zeelandia's father spoke many times of her mother, how special she was and how she had offered her own sacrifice to protect Arcadia from evil.

Zeelandia thought the childhood stories were fictional, stories designed to help grieving children deal with the loss of their loved ones. She never dreamed to think that it was a real place or that her mother was really someone special in the eyes of the council, that she had great powers or that indeed she may once again get to see her.

Inchinnan went on to say, *"Zeelandia, you will be taken far away from here, and with the help of Ballantine you will transcend space and time to spend time with the spirits of Arcadia, the greatest sorcerers and White Queens our land has ever witnessed. They will over the next seven days prepare you for the monumental challenges ahead.*

"You, my dear, are our only hope; with you the fate not only of Arcadia but of the entire universe rests; a heavy burden indeed, my child."

Zeelandia was indeed her mother's daughter, strong and pure of heart, and although she had been offered much protection so far, she was not aware that time and destiny would eventually immortalise her as the greatest White Queen Arcadia had ever borne.

Ballantine stood upright and looked directly at Zeelandia, *"Come, my child, we must prepare you for your journey into the land of the spirits — we have not one single moment to waste; as we speak, Vandermortel is already gathering powerful allies to help him in his quest to gain freedom."*

Zeelandia, without thought, fear or indeed contemplation, arose from her chair, gently kissed Kingston on the cheek and bid him farewell; she knew she had to remain strong, if indeed she were the only hope in preventing Vandermortel's escape.

This was not the time for fruitless emotion; she needed to remain strong, summon up all of the courage she could muster from within her very soul and meet the challenges that would undoubtedly seek her out, head on.

Ballantine and Zeelandia walked to the far wall in the chamber; Ballantine placed her right hand against the pale grey wall. Immediately a doorway appeared, adorning a thick oak door, hung by three large black hinges. To the left of the door was a golden lion's head about the size of a large man's hand, which was clearly the handle. Ballantine knocked three times on the door with her bare hand and once again spoke in ancient Arcadian: *"Saroso, Temporo, Alfeeto, Domaneta."* After a few seconds the door handle started to move of its own accord, it turned clockwise one full circle and the door gently creaked open.

Behind the door nothing could be seen; only darkness enshrouded the room beyond. Ballantine moved forward through the door and gestured for Zeelandia to follow, which she did without hesitation. The reflection from Ballantine's dress was the only source of light within the room ahead.

Once they were beyond the door a narrow corridor meandered off to the right. Suddenly, the door crashed closed behind them, and the room was pitched into complete darkness.

Zeelandia was not scared, not even concerned; she stood motionless; only the light whisper of her breath pierced the eerie silence within the room. She knew she was there for a reason and would without hesitation put all of her faith and trust in Ballantine and what was about to happen to her.

Vandermortel Prepares

Deep in the tall dark pine forest an area had been prepared. The clearing gave way to ten ancient upright pillars, two sets of four and one set of two. The two sets of four were laid out as adjacent squares with the two single pillars set as a diagonal between them.

In the centre of the space a large grey stone covered the ground, supporting each of the upright structures. The top of each pillar had been hand-carved and hollowed out, giving each the appearance of a turret affixed to a castle spire; each one had been set alight, sending dancing, enchanting, mesmerising flames high into the night sky.

The Gateway Stone had been placed in the centre of the space and was closely guarded by Solway.

Surrounding the stage, the silhouettes of the dark riders could be seen as far as the eye could see, spreading deep into the forest until their very shape was being blended into the bleak, dark and sinister scenery, disappearing into the night and out of sight.

Solway picked up a large branch from the ground beside him and banged it on the structure's floor three times.

The whole forest fell silent immediately. *"Bring the egrath to the altar,"* Solway bellowed.

Egraths were of a similar shape to humans; when fully grown they stand four metres high, they have two hearts and two brains, one heart and brain in their head, and another set in their upper torso.

The bound creature was dragged by six dark riders to the altar and thrown onto the ground in front of Solway and his master, who watched patiently, still bound by the confines of the Gateway Stone.

A piece of stone almost the same shape as an anvil was delivered by another dark rider. Solway lifted the egrath and forced his neck against the anvil. He then reached down and pulled his long shimmering sword from its sheath. With one flashing movement he sliced through the egrath's neck and decapitated the creature.

The head was thrown into the crowd, which immediately started a riot. Dark riders were fighting with each other, knives drawn; they were desperate for a piece of the egrath. The head was pulled and ripped apart with lumps of flesh torn from the head and every last piece devoured. Those dark riders who perished during the scramble were also torn apart and eaten in a horrific, primeval, cannibalistic, gluttonous show of basic instinct.

Solway forced the egrath to kneel in front of him. He lifted the Gateway Stone containing his master and placed the stone on top of the egrath's neck.

The whole area erupted into an electrifying display. White lights circumvented the Gateway Stone, like mini lightning strikes; beads of light bounced back and forth, and a white mist filled the stone.

After a short while, the lightning display ended and the mist slowly cleared. Vandermortel stood up, shook Solway's hand and turned to face his loyal disciples.

At the top of the egrath's body where its head had been just a few moments before, the Gateway Stone had somehow become attached and all that could be seen from within it was Vandermortel's head.

Vandermortel spoke to his followers. *"This is but the beginning of our journey. I am not yet free, but that day will soon be upon us, and you shall be well rewarded for your loyalty.*

"Using this egrath, I can once again walk amongst you, lead you and have the freedom to shape our destiny."

Vandermortel raised his right hand skyward and clenched his left fist, folding it across his chest. Looking out towards his disciples, he shouted: *"Tomorrow begins a new chapter in our history, but tonight you will feast, gorge yourselves and enjoy."*

The whole forest erupted amongst shouts and screams, cages were opened, thousands upon thousands of panwas were pulled from the cages and ripped apart, eaten raw, blood dripping; discarded remains were thrown aside, bones licked clean.

It was brutal savagery at its worst, but the behaviour did in fact depict in many ways the hideous, despicable creatures that were the dark riders of the apocalypse.

Long thin bony fingers at the end of skeletal arms. Faces hidden beneath hooded cloaks protected onlookers from the disfigured caricatures beneath; long pointed noses adorned a bony skeletal structure of a head, two eyes set close together; black and lifeless, sharp, pointed teeth protruded from a lipless orifice of a mouth, with no ears and no hair; they were a true depiction of hell itself.

The carnage lasted well into the night before finally the last of the dark riders had satisfied himself and fallen asleep. The forest at last fell silent.

For Vandermortel and Solway there was no time to partake in such frivolous activities, as they had little enough time to prepare for the journey and battles that lay ahead.

Vandermortel rose to his feet; he stood upright in the centre of the diagonal between the two vertical square columns. He raised both hands skyward and began to recite a phrase over and over again. *"Catasa, saframanta, cumosupreneo, toomokeh!"* Soon the dark skies turned red. White bolts of lightning ricocheted across the sky, and a whirling, whistling wind began to build up; slowly at first, quickly raging on and on until it reached a powerful crescendo, ripping up trees, boulders and everything in its path; finally, the ground began to shake, harder and harder, ripping a large gaping hole in front of the very area they were standing on.

A white mist started to appear from the crater. It slowly enveloped the whole area, and then suddenly the deafening noise ended as quickly as it had begun, soon replaced by a stagnant eerie silence.

Gradually, the mist began to clear, and when it had, three concrete statues were visible, levitating just above the open ground.

The first statue was that of an imposing lion, adorning a pair of gigantic outstretched wings.

The second was of a three-headed rhinoceros and the third a giant bird-like creature, not unlike a terradactyl, but over three times the size.

The lion was Galphia. He ruled over the planet Grator, several solar systems and many light years away from Arcadia. In ancient scripture Adelphi, Zeelandia's mother, turned the creature to stone as he wreaked havoc over the universe much in the same way that Vandermortel had been doing when he was stopped by Zeelandia.

The same was true of the rhinoceros; his name was Jeerplah. He played an important part in the age of darkness all those years before. He had led huge land armies of mythical creatures in support of Galphia and the quest to rule the universe.

Degla, the giant bird reptile, ruled the skies and protected Galphia, Jeerplah and his allies from above. Under his control were evil and abhorrent flying creatures and giant dragons.

During the final battle with Adelphi all three were turned to stone and buried under the mountains of Creed, the place where Vandermortel now stood.

Vandermortel once again spoke out. *"Galphia, Jeerplah and Degla, I have raised you from your mountain grave. I know you can hear me from within your concrete shroud. I, and I alone, can set you free.*

"If you promise to serve me in my quest to transcend the four kingdoms to the Mountains of Dean and raise your armies in my defence, then you shall have your freedom.

"If your heart is honest and your answer true when the lightning strikes, you will be free."

Vandermortel raised his hands above his head and looked skyward.

He recited the same rhyme as before: *"Catasa, saframanta, cumosupreneo, toomokeh."*

Quietly at first, his recital gradually got louder and louder until his voice bellowed out the words.

The sky became very dark; beads of white light emanated from his fingertips and rose into the night sky; bead after bead after bead, upwards searching out the heavy clouds above.

Each bead made a resounding crack as it collided with the clouds above; the display went on and on, each resounding crack getting louder and louder until the noise was perpetual and the intensity and depth of the sound almost unbearable.

Suddenly, three separate bolts of lightning came rushing groundward and simultaneously they struck the three stone statues that stood proud before Vandermortel.

The area once again fell silent, and for several moments nothing stirred at all.

Suddenly, the grey stone around the head of Galphia began to crack. The crack got bigger and wider, longer; it was like watching a new born chick hatch. Within a few moments Galphia flapped his wings, hovered free of the stone cask that had imprisoned him for many years and dropped down beside Vandermortel.

Galphia spoke in a very deep, low, growling voice. *"Vandermortel, raaaaaah, you have set me free and as promised, I will serve you, raaaaaah, in your quest to transcend the four kingdoms that lie before you, raaaaaah, to your journey's end at Mount Fleming.*

"I have been cocooned within that concrete blanket for far too long, but I am strong, and my armies wait to be called, raaaaaah."

"Galphia, you are indeed a legend, and all of those who support the dark side and who have followed the sacred

scriptures know only too well of your powers and the part you have played in defining history.

"It is indeed a great honour to have you by my side in this quest, along with Jeerplah and Degla; between us the dark side will once again take control of the universe and destroy Arcadia once and for all."

Simultaneously, the rocks around both Jeerplah and Degla began to crumble, turning to dust and falling on the dry stony ground. Both Jeerplah and Degla moved towards Galphia and Vandermortel.

Degla was the first to speak, in a loud, resounding, high-pitched voice. "I thank you for awakening me from that torture and for my freedom. I will serve you, lord, with every breath in my body." With that the giant bird reptile bowed his head and then moved to stand behind Galphia.

Jeerplah moved towards Vandermortel; his size and weight sent a resounding shudder through the ground with every step he took. In the deepest of all voices, he said, "I stand behind you, Vandermortel, and my previous master Galphia. Where you go, I go." He then moved to stand with the other two.

Vandermortel turned to the three comrades and bowed his head. "The ancient scriptures depict your immense battles with Arcadia and Adelphi, and you are a true inspiration to all who support the dark side and all that we stand for.

"For many years, whist imprisoned within the Gateway Stone, I have had time to plan my escape and the rise once again of the cause we all hold so dear.

"To have you three by my side will ensure our success and when I am free, together we can take on the might of Arcadia, and this time succeed in destroying all that they stand for. They will be no match for us."

Vandermortel turned to face his three new allies. *"Tonight, we must make haste with our plans. Let us form council round this obelisk and set in stone our strategy for success.*

"We have waited a long time, my friends; this is our time, a time for the dark side to rise once more, concur and destroy Arcadia.

"In the history of all that has gone before, there has never been a greater unity of power than that which sits around this table tonight. United we will be unstoppable, and great riches await all of us when we are triumphant."

Galphia, Jeerplah and Degla roared their seal of approval and stood beside their new lord and master.

Galphia turned to Vandermortel and in his deep, growling voice reaffirmed his commitment to the cause and expressed his desire to make haste with the planning for the battles ahead.

Zeelandia and the Journey to "The Spirits of Arcadia"

When Zeelandia's eyes finally adjusted to the light, her focus was drawn to a large chamber constructed from crystal.

The shimmering walls totally surrounded her; the colours flickered from white to pale blue, light pinks and glistening silver, ever changing, ever moving, mesmerising and captivating, drawing her closer and closer.

The walls themselves were smooth, but hanging from the ceiling, stalactites peeped downward, some very small, some searching deep into the chamber, almost touching the ground around her.

To her left-hand side, a small archway led into a lesser chamber in size, but not in importance; from where Zeelandia was standing she could not make out what lay behind the obscured entrance ahead.

Zeelandia barely felt Ballantine's hand on hers; for a moment she had almost forgotten that she was not alone.

Ballantine turned to Zeelandia. *"We have reached the Chamber of Destiny. It is bound by the souls of Arcadia, and the crystals from which it is formed capture all that is good.*

These crystals form the gateway to the spirits of Arcadia, and by becoming as one with them, you will transcend space and time and your spirit will be in unity."

Zeelandia had many questions, but immediately subdued her urge to ask; she knew deep down all that needed to be answered would be answered in good time.

"Firstly, Zeelandia, we must prepare you for the journey ahead, and for the experiences you shall encounter. Our greatest White Queens make this journey only once; they are immortalised forever but they can never return.

"You will transcend the two worlds and come back to us stronger, wiser and with a heart so pure that you shall have the strength, the courage and the wisdom to take on the might of Vandermortel and his allies. Put your trust in me.

"My task is to prepare you for the journey ahead.

"It will take us three encounters with the spirit world before you can take that final step. When you reach the spirit world, I will lose all contact with you, but fear not, child, I will be waiting for you on your return.

"No one has ever attempted to transcend the two worlds in the history of Arcadia, but it is written in the sacred scriptures that one day, when the world grows so dark and is in such mortal danger from the dark side, the greatest White Queen ever will rise and with a heart so pure will make that sacred journey.

"I fear we have now reached that time, and our future and that of the entire universe lies within this prophecy and our faith in you."

Zeelandia was still unable to speak; it was all too much to take in. So many thoughts were racing around her head.

How did anyone know that she was this person? What if she made the journey, but couldn't return? What if she simply wasn't strong enough to fulfil what was expected of her? Her head was spinning!

Ballantine turned to Zeelandia. *"I can hear all of your questions, my dear, and in good time you shall have all the answers you seek. All I ask is that you put your faith and trust in me, and we shall begin your first teachings."*

Ballantine continued. *"Over the next few days, you will make many journeys without leaving this sacred place. The Chamber of Destiny will reveal the secrets to all that remains unanswered and will provide the pathway for your journey ahead."*

Ballantine led Zeelandia through the archway and into the chamber beyond.

What appeared to be a glass or crystal bed lay perfectly in the middle of the room. The bed was adorned by one single white silk sheet and a pillow contained within a white silk pillowcase.

At the far end of the room two glass chairs straddled an open fire, the flames flickering and dancing mesmerisingly against the crystal walls of the chamber, the colours shimmering and pirouetting all around, bringing perspective and warmth to the room.

A small glass table stood beside and adjacent to one of the chairs.

On the opposite side of the room, but still within the chamber, an area had been set aside for the growing of plants, flowers and what appeared to be herbs.

Purples, yellows, blues and whites were the dominant colours trying to hide amongst a lush deep green carpet of leafy foliage.

Ballantine turned to Zeelandia. *"For all that you may not feel tired, my dear, it is time for you to rest. I must prepare you for your first lesson and for your first journey amongst the spirits."*

Zeelandia didn't question Ballantine or what she was saying. She gently pulled back the white silk sheet covering the bed. She lay down on her back, pulled the sheet up to her neck and after resting her head on the pillow, fell immediately into a deep, deep sleep.

Ballantine walked over to the garden area and carefully plucked a selection of petals from several of the plants.

She placed the petals into a mortar and began to grind them down with a pestle until they formed a very light, rust-coloured grainy mixture.

Next, she pulled out a small glass bottle from beneath her robe, she pulled gently on the cork stopper and the bottle opened with a tiny pop.

She carefully poured a minute amount of the opaque liquid into the mortar and stirred the mixture together.

When mixed, it produced a very small quantity of a light blue liquid which Ballantine emptied into a small crystal glass and placed on the table beside one of the chairs adjacent to the fire.

Ballantine walked into a third chamber and returned a few moments later, holding an intricately embossed book.

On its front cover the four corners to the forward-facing page had delicately crafted silver edges. Carvings depicting the silhouettes of many of Arcadia's great White Queens covered the rest of its shell, front and back, each one carefully hand crafted from rolled gold, delicate to the touch and just as precious as the contents of the book itself.

Ballantine turned the pages, one after another, and finally settled on a page she was happy with. She marked the page with a silver feather-shaped bookmark, closed the book and placed it on the table next to the glass containing the mixture.

After composing herself, she raised her robe above her knees, she knelt down in front of the table and opened the book to the page she had previously selected.

Ballantine held the crystal glass in her left hand and started to stir the mixture with a golden spoon held carefully in her other hand.

Glancing down to the book, she began to read from the scripture that stood prominent on the page and which was written in ancient Arcadian.

"Tempora, calidio resporo calacanti quewah."

She continued to stir the mixture, and after a few seconds a light blue mist started to form around the rim of the glass.

Ballantine removed the spoon from the mixture, but with its own momentum the liquid continued to spin gently round and round within the glass.

Slowly the mist disappeared and the mixture came to rest. Ballantine placed the glass back on the table, closed the precious book and returned it back to the third chamber.

As she returned, Zeelandia began to awake from her sleep and found Ballantine sitting on one of the chairs next to the fire.

She arose up from the bed and made her way across the room, taking up her allotted place on the second chair.

"I hope you are well rested, Zeelandia? As we are about to begin your first lesson."

"I am, thank you," Zeelandia replied.

Ballantine began to explain what would happen next and attempted to outline the experiences Zeelandia would encounter during this first occurrence.

She explained that this first journey would be a very short one, one in which she would get used to leaving her mortal body and spiritually transcending space and time.

Ballantine urged Zeelandia to take a sip from the glass and then return to her bed. This Zeelandia did without question.

At first Zeelandia felt nothing at all; then slowly, she felt a slight tingling sensation flow through her body, from her toes, up through her legs, along her arms and finally a warm, glowing feeling passed over her head.

She lost all feeling in her body — she felt numb; she had no control over any of her bodily functions; she found herself hovering just above the bed, looking down at her own figure below, apparently still fast asleep.

She was levitating just above the bed, arms outstretched. Zeelandia had no idea what was happening to her.

She had no control over anything. All she could do was watch, listen and try to focus on her surroundings.

The figure lying on the bed began to quiver. Her head was moving back and forth. Zeelandia didn't know what to make of the experience; she had no idea what was happening with her body below and she had no power to do anything but to watch, isolated from above.

Beads of light effervesced from the figure below, engulfing her entire body, dancing round and round.

Zeelandia started shaking uncontrollably; she was shouting out Vandermortel's name along with those of Galphia, Jeerplah and Degla. Suddenly, she sat bolt upright on the bed, eyes wide open and screamed out loud her mother's name: *"Adelphi — Adelphi."* She awoke with a start. She was no longer hovering above the bed; she had rejoined her body, and they were as one together again.

Ballantine approached Zeelandia and placed her arms around her, comforting her and helping her regain a sense of perspective and focus her on where she was.

"Zeelandia, you have had your first encounter with the spirit world, but to complete your first lesson you must convey your experience and your learning to me."

Zeelandia was still a little confused; she described the feeling of levitation, of leaving her body.

The spirits had not all been good; she recalled her last encounter with Vandermortel, and his spirit had haunted her during the sleep.

There were also strange creatures by the side of Vandermortel that she had never seen before. They were taunting and ridiculing her; they said she would pay the price for the actions of her mother, and for the suffering they had endured at her hands.

Then a single white light flashed before her, drove the dark spirits away, and she awoke from her sleep.

"That is a good start, Zeelandia; the first lesson is about leaving and rejoining your physical body, which you have done, recognised and understood; unfortunately, we cannot control the spirits of the dark side and how they will attempt to interfere with your lessons.

"However, they are not present in a physical way, so they cannot hurt you at all; you will grow stronger and learn to block them from your mind as our lessons continue."

Zeelandia turned to Ballantine and asked her about the experience. *"Who were these creatures by Vandermortel's side and what did they mean when they talked about my mother?"*

Ballantine went on to explain that Vandermortel had conjured up Galphia, Jeerplah and Degla and explained how her mother had defeated them in battle and turned them to stone. They were now free and would support Vandermortel in his bid for freedom.

"The white light that awoke you was the spirit of Adelphi, your mother.

"In time you will come to recognise her. She has confirmed her presence and will guide you through the rest of your teachings.

"Tomorrow we will explore further the spirit world. You will undertake your second lesson; you will travel further, longer and come back stronger and another step closer to making your ultimate journey."

Whilst Zeelandia lay sleeping Ballantine again disappeared into the third chamber.

On a small round table sat a crystal ball. Ballantine placed her hands on the ball and addressed the ball in ancient Arcadian. *"Deri, stamori, cabana, deliofractus, suporo."* —

The ball responded by misting up, then instantaneously clearing to show the head of the most beautiful of women. Long golden hair, powder blue eyes and a complexion so fair.

Ballantine spoke to the ball. *"Adelphi, we have taken the first steps in reuniting you with your daughter. Tomorrow we* shall begin the second lesson, and when the third is complete, Zeelandia will join you and the spirits of Arcadia.

"She is strong and pure of heart and puts her trust in learning".

"Thank you, Ballantine," Adelphi replied. "This is a dangerous thing that we do, and it is with a heavy heart that it has become necessary. You know what must be done, and it is with haste that we must now act."

Ballantine bid farewell to Adelphi and moved her hand over the ball, which immediately returned to its innate form.

Ballantine again removed the black book from the chamber, sat on the chair in the next room and began to fastidiously flick through its pages.

She selected the required page and lay the open book on the table and again moved across and picked a few leaves from selected plants.

Once again, she mixed and ground the chosen ingredients with a small quantity of liquid from the same small glass bottle she had used before, mixed it well and tipped it into another crystal glass.

Using the golden spoon, she stirred the mixture and as before recited the same phrase: "Tempora, calidio resporo calacanti quewah".

Again, the mixture permeated a mist around the glass, this time turning a light shade of the palest green before dissipating and leaving once more a clear mixture in the glass.

The book was once again returned to the third chamber, and Ballantine returned to sit on one of the chairs.

Zeelandia approached and spoke to Ballantine. "I can see you have prepared a fresh potion for me. Does that mean it is now time for my second encounter with the spirit world?"

"Indeed, it does, my child, but this time you will be away for much longer and you will grow in strength and character; please take a sip from the glass and return to your bed."

Zeelandia did as she was instructed; this time the feeling of incapacitation was almost instantaneous. She felt herself once again levitate above the bed, but this time there was no experience of watching from above; she was experiencing something quite extraordinary from within.

She started to spin, faster and faster, uncontrollably, flying through the air, through space, through time.

Stopping; instantaneously capturing pictures in her mind. Hillsides, dark riders, sunshine, her mother, fields of buttercups, Vandermortel, images, pictures of different lands and planets — a kaleidoscope of different colours all merging into one.

Pulled to the edge of a precipice and then pulled back, a sense of falling uncontrollably to the ground, excitement, euphoria and sadness all rolled into one.

She felt herself laughing, crying, screaming and shouting, but at what? By the time her emotion had caught up with that moment, the picture in her mind had already moved on, and she was looking at something new.

Then, without warning, she could see her mother standing in front of her, looking, speaking, but she couldn't hear her, she couldn't make herself heard; she felt herself being torn away.

The motion slowed down, the spinning disappeared and she felt herself fall gently back onto the bed.

When she awoke, she found Ballantine sitting on the bed beside her.

"There is no need to explain your encounter. I have journeyed it with you. You are growing stronger, and when tomorrow's lesson is complete, you shall be ready to join the spirits."

On the third day Zeelandia knew exactly what to expect. The potion had already been prepared for her and was waiting beside Ballantine on the table.

Zeelandia took one sip from the glass and immediately fell once more into unconsciousness. She became one with the swirling flames from the fire and rose skyward as though lifted by the heat.

She felt herself flying, arms outstretched, passing the many stars that adorned the night sky.

Passing many worlds, some known to her, some written about in ancient scriptures and some that looked like the most dark and desolate places imaginable.

Suddenly, Zeelandia felt comfort from her left-hand side. She looked round to find herself holding hands with her mother, Adelphi, being guided and shown the secrets of the universe. Nothing was said, but a deep learning and understanding of all things good and evil filled her mind and her body.

The journey continued; it was as though she was soaking up the past, its history, the beginnings of time and the role of Arcadia, but more importantly, a deep understanding of her own destiny and the part she had to play in what was to come.

This was only the start; there would be far more for her to absorb and to learn from.

Zeelandia awoke as quickly as she had fallen asleep, if indeed that was what had actually happened to her. Ballantine was, of course, sitting by her side.

Zeelandia turned to Ballantine, *"Now I know what my destiny is; somehow I understand far more than I ever knew. I don't know how I have come to gain this knowledge or indeed its extent, but somehow I feel that I have a part to play, and my destiny is already written."*

"You are correct, my child; tomorrow your final journey will see you transcend space and time, and you will join Adelphi and the other great spirits of Arcadia. You will return a great White Queen and be a force for good, but for now go and rest."

Zeelandia headed to her chamber to rest and to try to comprehend what was happening to her, to gather stock and to think in detail about what had passed and what was yet to come.

By now Zeelandia knew the routine only too well.

Ballantine approached her slowly. Turning to Zeelandia, she spoke to her in a hushed voice. *"Before you can make this journey you must dress as the White Queen you now are. You have great powers, my child, far more than you may realise at present, but you will not be recognised at the gateway to the spirits of Arcadia if you are not dressed appropriately.*

"For those who try to enter and do not adorn these sacred robes are invisible to the spirits and will not be allowed to enter."

Ballantine led Zeelandia into the third chamber. On the far wall standing on its own was a flowing white gown, covered in diamonds and pearls.

Ballantine assisted Zeelandia into the gown, which fitted perfectly. With a high white neckline, perfectly cut, it flowed down over her waist, stopping level with her ankles.

Ballantine reached into a silver box lying on a table and took out a diamond-encrusted tiara and placed it on top of Zeelandia's head.

"Now, my child, you are truly a White Queen and you are ready to make this final sacred journey."

This time there was no requirement for potions. Zeelandia walked into the bedroom chamber, she walked over to the fire and for the first time spoke quietly in ancient Arcadian.

"Flapooray, whatoso queasatay santamoro paparoki."

Suddenly and without warning, the fire extinguished, the crystal roof parted, and a bright light shone down on Zeelandia from above.

Her body was drawn into the light and lifted effortlessly, clear of the structure; instantaneously, she disappeared into the night sky as though sucked into eternity, gone in an instant.

Zeelandia felt herself cocooned within a white sphere; again, a kaleidoscope of pastel shades — blues, greens, pinks, creams flickered before her.

She found herself motionless, rotating within the sphere, travelling on and on.

The journey was long, yet appeared short at the same time. Zeelandia was safe contained within the sphere, but felt very vulnerable.

She had put her faith in Ballantine, and now found herself embarking on a journey, not knowing where it would take her or where it would end.

Without warning, the sphere stopped rotating; arriving at its destination, it came to rest suddenly.

The sphere slowly opened. Zeelandia found herself sitting on a silver throne in a large, light and airy room.

Around the room she could see many thrones, all occupied by similarly dressed figures. At the end of the room, at the head of a large table, she instantly recognised the figure of her mother, Adelphi.

Adelphi arose from her throne and walked towards her daughter.

"My dearest Zeelandia, welcome to the Great Council of Arcadia. There is much that we need to talk about and much that we must accomplish, if we are to succeed in the coming battles with Vandermortel, his allies and indeed with the might of the dark side.

"For the time being, I will introduce you to each of the members of the Great Council, the true spirits of Arcadia."

The Council and the Four Lords Prepare

Inchinnan looked across the large oval table towards Kingston and Bridgewater, bowing his head. The three had just witnessed the enchanted wall reveal the second coming of Galphia, Jeerplah and Degla and they knew this was not good news.

Inchinnan spoke in a quiet, but quite resolute voice. *"My friends, this is our worst fear. Vandermortel will be challenge enough for Zeelandia, but to have these three dark powers as his allies, Zeelandia's task will be ever more difficult."*

Inchinnan had been party to the battles of old when these three adversaries joined forces to try to defeat Arcadia and all that it stood for.

He had been at Adelphi's side when she conquered over the three and turned them to stone.

These three in their own right were great, and powerful sorcerers, committed to the dark side and to the destruction of good.

It had taken the full force of Arcadia's greatest White Queen to defeat the three. The task had been long and hard, the battles ferocious, and not without sacrifice. It had cost

Adelphi her mortal life and saw her taken to the land of the spirits.

Inchinnan had summoned the kings of the four kingdoms to form an emergency council; they had much to do in preparation for the battles to come. Inchinnan stood up and turned to Kingston and Bridgewater:

"My friends, the four kings await us in the adjoining chamber. We will have many long nights ahead of us as we prepare to do battle with the dark side." Inchinnan placed his hand on the wall of the chamber and immediately an opening appeared; he walked through the opening, beckoning Kingston and Bridgewater to follow, which they did.

As they entered the chamber, the opening closed immediately behind them. In the room another large oak table adorned the room. The table was circular in shape. Already seated at the table were four figures.

Inchinnan turned to the figures and bowed his head in their direction. *"My lords, this is a desperate time in our history. As you are aware, Vandermortel will attempt to transcend each of your kingdoms in a bid to reach the Mountains of Dean. We must do all in our power to stop this from happening — otherwise the rise of the dark side will gather momentum, strength and purpose.*

"We will witness via the enchanted wall Vandermortel as he sits with his new-found allies and plots his strategy. It is with a heavy heart, however, that I must divulge the identities of these new allies.

Vandermortel has resurrected Galphia, Jeerplah and Degla and at this moment they sit by his side."

The room was silent. *"Before we begin our council, I will introduce Kingston and Bridgewater to you."*

The first to be introduced was Xanti. He was the lord and ruler over Citronus, the first land that Vandermortel would have to transcend during his journey ahead.

The Citronic people were as dwarfs, short, stocky people with great strength. They were a fighting breed, with the heart of a lion and courage to match.

The great scriptures of old paid enormous debts of gratitude to the people of Citronus for their service to Arcadia and the hard battles they had fought against evil in support of the free world.

The second was Astrolis, the last Dragon Master; he ruled over the ancient land of dragons and watched over the dragon spirits of that land.

Testament had it that Astrolis and his dragons had watched over Arcadia and contributed significantly when helping Adelphi succeed in the battle against Galphia, Jeerplah, but more importantly against Degla in times gone by.

Third was Trevelous, a slight figure of a man. A great sorcerer and long-time friend of Arcadia. He presided over the spiritual land known as Garouvious.

A land previously filled with ancient woodland where it was said that the trees, when summoned, come alive to fend off evil spirits.

The land long lost to the dark powers of the past, where the once green landscape was now scorched bare and volcanic activity permeates the entire landscape.

Trevelous had the power to summon up the great spirits of nature and the dead spirits of his dead ancestors and use the elements of nature to help protect his allies.

Finally, Kingston and Bridgewater were introduced to the fourth and final lord; her name was Insignia, ruler over the

Solomon Forest, a land where elves and fairies danced amongst the meadows and woodlands.

They were known as a gentle people, but not devoid of conflict in the past, and capable of great things when called upon. Never a people to be underestimated, and although gentleness and conflict avoidance lay at the heart of their souls, when required, they too become great and feared warriors.

They were as one with the great forest they called home.

"Now that we have the introductions out of the way, we must with haste determine the actions we will take if we are to succeed in stopping Vandermortel from reaching Mount Fleming." Inchinnan gestured to Bridgewater and Kingston, inviting them to sit down at the table. Inchinnan then took up his place at the table's head.

All of them knew that this was not going to be an easy task, especially now that Vandermortel had three of the dark side's most powerful advocates by his side.

The council had to try to second guess Vandermortel, who himself with the dark riders would be a match for any army. But with the assistance of Galphia, Degla, and Jeerplah, it was difficult to imagine what force Vandermortel would rain down on them, and how they could even contemplate by what power they could stop him.

The council members initially sat in silence. The first to speak in a quiet, assured voice was Trevelous. *"It is indeed a dark place that we find ourselves in, and I for one am unsure, even with the purity of heart sat around this table today, how we can we even contemplate stopping Vandermortel from succeeding in his quest.*

"We can resist his progress and we can all sacrifice greatly for the cause, but I fear our resistance will in the end prove futile."

Xanti hit back, almost outraged by this suggestion. The small dwarf whose fighting spirit could not be hidden and whose anger at the thought of Vandermortel being freed was plain for everyone to see.

"My people will fight with every breath in their body to stop Vandermortel and his new allies succeeding, and if destiny should have us die in the process, then that is a sacrifice my people and I are willing to make.

"For many decades now, the universe and each of our lands has flourished without interference from the dark side, but like all of us sitting round this table, we can all remember the death and destruction rained down upon us in the past by this evil."

Trevelous interjected, *"My friend Xanti, I am not for one moment suggesting we do nothing. I am simply stating what is obvious for all of us to see, and we must all be prepared to make the same sacrifices, even if in the end it is to no avail.*

"I and my people, like the entire universe, have suffered at the hands of the dark side. We have all made sacrifices in the past and we will once again readily stand up and give everything to the cause. But we must remain mindful of what that may mean."

Inchinnan was the next to speak. *"Zeelandia, with the assistance of Ballantine, has journeyed to Arcadia to sit with the great White Queens of the past, including Adelphi, and as we speak, sits beside the spirits of Arcadia; with her a great deal of our faith, trust and hope must rest.*

"Trevelous, you may well be correct, and all that we may succeed in doing by fighting these mortal battles will be to slow down Vandermortel's journey to Mount Fleming. The longer that journey takes, the more time we will give to Zeelandia, for her to learn her craft and prepare from our great White Queens and sorcerers of the past.

"She may well be the only one who can truly take on the combined might of Vandermortel, Galphia, Degla, and Jeerplah. But if our fate is for us to make the ultimate sacrifice in order for her to take up that battle, then I, for one, am happy to make that commitment.

"Are we all in agreement?"

Each member of the council raised their hand in support. One by one they placed their hand on the table, one on top of each other and with a combined unity of purpose their commitment was pledged. *"Then let us make haste with our planning."*

The hours rolled into days and then nights; the council debated long and hard the best ways in which to resist the dark side, and what tactics they would deploy in the days ahead.

Although wielding great power, each of the lords' strengths lay only within the boundaries of their own kingdoms; so, their contribution and that of their people was restricted to their own lands.

The first battle would take place in the Kingdom of Citronus, and Xanti the Dwarf King would lead the defence of his kingdom.

This would prove to be a brutal, bloody battle, but it was indeed the only way that the people of Citronus knew how to fight.

Xanti stood up and walked to the front of the room. He picked up a small piece of white chalk and drew a map on the wall; he then turned and addressed his comrades, pointing a long stick at the drawing and gesturing as he spoke.

"Vandermortel, from where he now rests, will first transcend the flatlands to the west of the great valley, heading south towards the Caves of Citronus.

"This is no easy place for us to take on the might of his army; it is a wide-open area of grassland, with no shelter, or place from which to mount an unseen attack. Any conflict here will be bloody and not without great loss.

"However, if we assemble our army at the southern edge of the grasslands on the south-eastern border close to the caves, then we can make a strategic retreat into the caves and continue the battle from within. The advantage will then lie with us."

Astrolis interjected, *"This plan must be well thought through to ensure as few lives as possible are lost during this first encounter."*

Xanti hit back once more. *"Astrolis, here we go again — if we survive and Vandermortel is free, then we have no life; my people would rather die in combat than face that prospect."*

"That's not what I'm saying, Xanti, and I will gladly and without thought give up my life for the cause; but if Vandermortel does win his freedom and we all die, then he has won.

"We need to ensure that enough of our people from each of the four kingdoms survive and can once again grow and prepare to challenge him again at some point.

"We all feel as you do, but we must remain focused on doing what is best, not only now but for the future. We will be of no use to Zeelandia if we are all dead."

The group then continued to discuss the strategy for the first battle and their attention was again focused on Xanti.

"As I said, I will amass a great army of my people at the southern edge of the grasslands close to the caves. From there we will watch Vandermortel and his armies move across the grassland. As they approach the southern area, we will attack and engage with them.

"I will sound the retreat when we have achieved all that we can achieve, and we will fall back into the caves.

"If Vandermortel is to transcend the kingdom successfully, he will need to navigate his way through the long, narrow, winding passageways.

"It is within those passageways that my warriors will stand the best chance of taking on Vandermortel's dark riders."

The passageways were narrow, severely restricted in height, fashioned out of the hard rock many hundreds of years before by the first people of Citronus and used as their first line of defence in many encounters over the years.

The height of the passageways meant that anyone taller than the dwarfs who inhabited the caves would not be able to stand upright when passing through, but the people of Citronus, whose ingenuity had developed the cave system, could stand tall and fight off anyone who dared enter, maximising their clever defence system.

The meeting went on, surpassing the day and moving into the night, until finally the participants determined a strategy, they were all agreed upon.

They knew the likelihood of stopping Vandermortel's progress though each of the kingdoms was unlikely at best. However, they were happy that the decisions they had made would give them the greatest opportunity to slow him down, deplete his vast armies and give Zeelandia much needed time to prepare.

Xanti pulled his sword from its sheath and raised it above his head. *"My fellow warriors, let us make haste to Citronus and let us prepare for our first battle; we have little time to waste and we must prepare well."*

Zeelandia's First Teachings

Zeelandia arose from her throne and stood beside her mother; she held out her hand in front of her, and her mother placed her hand against it.

There was no emotion, no questions, no searching for answers, just a deep understanding that they were party to something quite special, something so deep, so spiritual that all emotion was rendered impotent.

There was no longing for the past, no intimacy between mother and daughter; this was simply a meeting of two great White Queens, one ready to impart knowledge and one eager to receive.

Adelphi led the way round the large table and approached the first of the White Queens. Zeelandia followed behind her. *"This is Arturios."*

Zeelandia bowed her head in Arturios's direction. Neither Zeelandia nor Arturios acknowledged the introduction. Adelphi quickly approached each of the thrones and one by one introduced each of them; after Sherideso, next to be introduced was Flymoro, and finally Heathrodece.

The whole room was silent. Adelphi turned to Zeelandia. *"We will go and sit for a while, and I will explain to you the nature of the teachings to follow, and how our knowledge shall be imparted."*

The pair turned, and Zeelandia followed Adelphi out of the room.

They walked along a narrow passageway, passing through many sets of doors before reaching an archway exuding a bright pearl white light.

"My dear Zeelandia, we shall enter the crypt of Arcadia, the spiritual heart of our land, where you will become as one with each of the great White Queens you have been introduced to. One by one their great knowledge and power will pass from them to you within this very crypt. When you leave the crypt for the last time, after sitting with me, you will have absorbed all of the power and knowledge available to you, and it is our hope that you will be strong enough to take on the might of Vandermortel and his allies once again.

"For now, let us enter the crypt and sit for a moment in silence."

Zeelandia followed Adelphi into the crypt. She could see two glass sculptures taking the shape of translucent thrones, sitting opposite one another in the middle of the room.

Separating the thrones, Zeelandia could see what appeared to be a neatly stacked pile of crystal rods carefully placed like kindling on a fire that was ready to be set alight.

Adelphi sat on one of the thrones, with Zeelandia quickly taking up her place alongside her on the other.

Adelphi picked up one of the crystal rods and handed it to Zeelandia; she then picked up another one for herself.

They each clasped the rods with one hand, leant forward and touched the remaining pile of rods in front of them and closed their eyes.

The room was silent. The light appeared to fade, and Zeelandia felt her thoughts drift in and out of her subconscious until her mind was totally clear.

Suddenly, from behind closed eyes, Zeelandia sensed the room brighten once again. She felt compelled to open her eyes.

When she did so, she could see the shape of Adelphi sitting on the throne opposite, already awake.

The crystal rod in her hand was shimmering, changing from light blue to pale yellow and then to bright white. It then settled back into its original character, translucent and clear.

"That was one of the most tranquil and peaceful moments in my life, Adelphi. I feel so relaxed and at one with myself here. I felt almost hypnotised and had not one single thought running through my head."

"That is the beauty of meditation within the crypt, Zeelandia; it allows us to clear our minds and consider things without the intrusion of thought, and it is through this meditation that your mind will be open to receiving the great knowledge that we must impart upon you.

"Time is of the essence, for tomorrow your teachings will begin; for now, I will take you to your sleeping chamber, a place for rest and recovery."

They both alighted from their great chairs and walked out of the crypt, with Zeelandia again following closely behind Adelphi. No words were spoken as they meandered back down the long corridor from where they had travelled a short while before.

Adelphi placed her hand on a large wooden door, which without any help opened slowly inward, revealing the chamber within.

Adelphi moved gracefully as though floating just above the ground into the chamber.

Once inside Zeelandia cast her eyes around the circular room. The walls and ceiling were pale blue in colour; it was difficult to see where the walls ended and the ceiling began.

In the centre of the room Zeelandia could see only one piece of furniture. A large four poster bed made out of glass, or crystal or some similar material.

The bed had no sheets, or covers; just one single pillow covered by a white pillowcase, lying gently at the head of the bed, positioned exactly in the middle of the translucent mattress.

At the top of each corner attached to the translucent uprights, a lush gathering of opulent fabric adorned the structure; a tapestry of pastel colours intermingled with one another giving a sense of warmth and tranquillity, peace and quiet, carefully attached to each of the four corners, lying ready to be released at a moment's notice and ready to steal away and hide, if required, the occupant within.

"Tonight, my child, rest well. Tomorrow a new chapter in the history of Arcadia will begin."

With that Adelphi turned around and walked through the open door, which closed effortlessly and of its own accord behind her.

Zeelandia sat on the edge of the bed; she had a million thoughts running through her head, wondering about the teachings to come and questioning if she were truly worthy of such great hope and trust.

She kicked off her shoes and lay on the bed, resting her head gently on the soft, gentle pillow.

As Zeelandia closed her eyes, she saw the fabric around the bed gently loosen and fall silently around the bed, screening her from the outside world, sending the room into complete darkness and ushering her into a deep but restless sleep.

When Zeelandia awoke, she was anxious and trembling uncontrollably; she felt as though she had been taken on a terrifying journey — she had witnessed many strange and horrible things: mythical creatures brought back from the dead, fighting, bloodshed, strange lands and flashbacks to her last encounter with Vandermortel.

Her thoughts lay with Lazonby and the cruel fate he had suffered at the hands of Solway.

Was it a dream? Was it fate? Was it a vision of what was to come? She tried to make sense of it; she tried to put her thoughts in order and focus on what she could remember about her dream.

Her mind was racing faster and faster; more thoughts focused and permeated her subconscious, then disappeared as quickly as they had appeared.

Suddenly she felt herself relax — her body was still; she'd stopped shaking.

Her thoughts clear and structured, she turned to her right to see Adelphi standing to the side of the bed.

She felt at peace; it was surreal, tranquil. She had in her mind a million images, but this time they all appeared to make perfect sense.

Zeelandia turned to Adelphi, but Adelphi spoke first. "*You have lain in the bed of prophecy; all that you have encountered* may not happen. *You have seen good and evil; some of what might be, and all that will become.*

"You have witnessed your destiny, my child. You have witnessed some of the choices you will have to make in the days ahead. But only the choices you make when faced with reality will shape what is to come."

Zeelandia spoke quietly. *"Mother, sorry Adelphi, I don't fully understand or comprehend what you are saying.*

"Surely if I have seen what lies ahead, then we can plan what we must do next. If only my choices shape the future and our destiny, then surely we can prepare and ensure I make the correct choices."

"I'm sorry, Zeelandia, if only it were that simple. You will be faced with many different encounters on your journey and your heart may lead you down many paths; numerous questions will be asked of you.

"Only when you are faced with the reality of each situation can you look deep into your own heart and decide upon which path to follow.

"Your decisions will be guided by the decisions and actions of others, not under your control.

"You are here with us to take on board our experiences and our learning from the past. We will journey with you on your quest through those teachings, and when you need us, when you search your heart for guidance, then we will be there for you.

"We are unable to give you the answers you seek, but we can open your heart to the possibilities ahead.

"Today your education begins in earnest, and the crypt has been made ready for your first teaching. Let us begin."

Preparation for the Battle for Citronus

Vandermortel's army was on the move; they marched constantly for three days and three nights without rest — they didn't need it; they moved ever closer to the flatlands between the Citronus ranges.

Led by Vandermortel, closely followed by Solway and Jeerplah with Degla and Galphia flying overhead, patrolling the landscape ahead of them.

Hundreds of thousands of dark riders brought up the rear with only bloodshed, battle and the spoils of war on their minds.

As predicted by Xanti, this colossal army convened to the west of the flatlands at the entrance to the gorge between the two sets of Citronus mountains which lay both to the north and south of their current position.

As the army halted, the whole ground shook and an intense wave vibrated through the earth, of a magnitude only imaginable. It spread across the land before them and could be felt by Xanti's opposing army assembling to the north of Mount Citronus at the entrance to the caves.

Xanti's army stood in formation at this point towards the very south of the grasslands and, although numbering tens of thousands deep itself, was shaken by the scale of the tremors that reverberated around them.

The caves had been fortified and made ready for both invasion and defence.

If Vandermortel and his allies were to navigate their way through these caves and out to the south of Citronus, they would be well on their way to where their second challenge and a battle with Astrolis awaited them.

Xanti stood upright. He had Astrolis, Trevelous and Insignia by his side — they would fight together this day, but Xanti knew that any sacrifices made would belong to him and his people alone.

Two menacing figures could be seen in the distance, soaring high in the clear blue skies above. They were a long way out, but Xanti was the first to confirm that the figures soaring high above were those of Galphia and Degla. This was a reconnaissance trip, not an engagement exercise; they were surveying the landscape before them, sizing up the strength of Xanti's army: the numbers, formation and precise location, eager to relay the information back to Vandermortel on their return.

Xanti's army was impressive, not in numbers alone, although they were significant.

They were well drilled, the formations looked solid and the line upon line of Citronus dwarfs filled the grasslands as far as the eye could see.

This would be no pushover for Vandermortel's army, despite heavily outnumbering the dwarfs. Vandermortel had long since learned not to underestimate the courage and fighting spirit of these proud people. They may well be small in stature, but they fought with the strength and determination of beings ten times their size.

They were resolute, brave and fought with valour — always.

Line upon line of dwarfs, shields ready, and a combination of swords, spears and axes to hand, waited silently, resolutely, for the battle to commence.

The four lords retreated from the front line, dismounted from their horses and stood at the entrance to the Caves of Citronus; this would be where the dwarf army really needed to take the fight to Vandermortel — take him on in the confines of their own cave networks and exploit their short physiques.

Xanti had two brothers, Tryson and Sharjay, and one son, Theagor. All three were waiting at the entrance to the caves, awaiting instruction from Xanti.

Dwarfs lived for about one hundred and fifty years. Xanti was the eldest — he was eighty-seven, his eldest brother Tryson was seventy-nine, about to turn eighty in three weeks' time, and his youngest brother Sharjay was seventy-two.

The youngest member of the family to be engaged in the battle to come was Xanti's son Theagor — he was a mere forty-two.

Xanti was very close to his brothers. Their father, Valert, had fallen in battle some fifty years previously as he defended Citronus from an attack by a number of Gelopodites, serpent-like creatures who frequent the mountain walls and could burrow through solid stone, who entered the kingdom of Citronus, seeking sanctuary.

They betrayed Valert's trust, and in the dark of night, mounted an attack on Citronus to lay claim to the mountain range for themselves.

Valert repelled the attack, and his army defeated the Gelopodites, slaying every last one of them; unfortunately, it cost him his life.

Xanti, a thirty-seven-year-old at the time, became the youngest leader of the Citronic people, and until this day he had yet to lift his sword in anger or have to defend Citronus in a way that was expected of him now.

"Brothers, and my son Theagor, today and the days ahead will mark a defining moment in the history of Citronus.

"We face a bloody battle in the grasslands, and we will defend these mountains with all our might — I will, however, not sacrifice one more person than I have to out in the open.

"If I sound the retreat, we will fall back into the caves and take the battle to Vandermortel on our terms.

"Tryson, I want you, Sharjay and Theagor, along with five hundred men to make your way through the caves to the Great Hall on the east side of the mountain and wait. Close the doors and barricade them behind you.

"If the caves are being overrun, Vandermortel and his dark riders will make their way past that position to the south passageway and on towards the land of dragons and Astrolis's kingdom.

"I have already assembled another five hundred men in the caves to the west. If you hear them engaged in battle, it means that Vandermortel has overrun our defences and is making good his escape from the mountain. On command your troops will fall in behind the dark riders and kill as many of them as possible — deplete his army as far as is achievable."

Theagor was the first to speak.

"Father, we want to stand by your side on the battlefield — not hide away like cowards in the caves."

Tryson and Sharjay mirrored Theagor's comments. Xanti raised his voice and clasped his son's head between his hands.

"Son, listen to me, we must all play our part today, but moreover, we must be here to carry on the fight past this day, if need be. I need you under the command of Tryson to carry out my instructions and follow the plan I have set — you will have your fair share of battle and bloodshed today, my son, of that I have no doubt.

"Tryson, take the men and go now and await my signal to engage." As the men moved out, Xanti grabbed Tryson by the forearm and whispered in his ear, *"Look after your brother and your nephew this day, above all other days. If you hear fighting outside the door to the chamber, do not exit the chamber until you hear my order — it is important that the dark riders journey beyond your position before you chase them down and engage in battle. Promise me!"*—

Tryson looked away. Xanti held onto his arm and wouldn't let go. *"Promise me, now; say it."*

"I promise — I promise," replied Tryson.

"Good — Let God be with you today, my brother."

Galphia and Degla swooped down from the sky, barely seen by the army amassed behind Vandermortel, and dropped to the ground just in front of him.

Jeerplah was standing to the left and just behind Vandermortel, Solway, as always, standing upright immediately to his master's right-hand side.

"What news do you bring me?" Vandermortel asked.

"*Just as you predicted,*" replied Galphia, "*Xanti has amassed his army to the south of the grasslands and protects the gateway to the caves of Mount Citronus.*

"*They are many in number but only a fraction of the numbers we have fighting for us today. They have beside them Astrolis, Trevelous and Insignia, but we saw no sign of Zeelandia.*"

Vandermortel remained silent for a few seconds, reflecting on the news he had just been given. "*We cannot wait for her to show herself; let us prepare to do battle — you all know the plan.*"

Vandermortel contemplated what he thought Zeelandia's next move might be; she had caught him out once before, and he was determined she would never get the better of him again.

How could she influence this battle; what power did she have over this situation; where was she?

Vandermortel had great powers himself, but he could not sense Zeelandia's physical or spiritual presence anywhere around; this was strange — something was not right.

He could not afford to drop his guard, not even for one single second.

The First Secrets of the White Queens

Zeelandia entered the crypt and took up her position in the glass chair adjacent to the column of crystal rods, directly in front of the second glass chair standing empty opposite her, just as she had done previously whilst sitting with her mother in the crypt a few days earlier.

This time she knew it was far more serious than anything she had ever done in the past, but she knew deep down that she was there for a reason; she had been chosen and she had to remain strong, resolute and deliver whatever was now expected of her.

Zeelandia waited patiently for several minutes; the door to the crypt opened silently, a long shadow cast eerily over the wall; in walked Arturios, the first great White Queen Zeelandia had been introduced to on her arrival in Arcadia.

All of the great White Queens were beautiful, elegant and so demure, but none more so than Arturios.

You could not determine age by her skin tone; her face was silky smooth: no wrinkles, marks, blemishes — she was ageless. Powder blue eyes, almost iridescent, long flowing blond hair falling just below her shoulders, she adorned a crisp white dress, encrusted with precious stones, too numerous to mention or describe.

The dress she wore flowed from her shoulders, wrapping tightly around her narrow waist and flowed gently down, wrinkleless to the floor — she was indeed the incarnation of beauty itself.

However, hidden below this tranquil exterior lay a great White Queen, a fearless warrior and sorceress who had herself faced down the might of the dark side centuries ago and one who had earned her place in Arcadian history; her place as a great White Queen, a legend, had been immortalised by those who followed her and made sure she was depicted in the sacred scriptures of times gone by as such.

At first Arturios did not speak; she sat down in the chair opposite Zeelandia, bowed her head and closed her eyes.

Zeelandia was entranced; she couldn't take her eyes off her.

Arturios opened her eyes and lifted her head; Zeelandia tried to avert her glaze — she didn't want to be caught staring at her, but was too slow, caught in the act, but no mention of it by Arturios, who remained calm, focused and well prepared for the encounter they were about to have.

Zeelandia wished the same could be said for her.

Arturios spoke gently, sensing Zeelandia's unease. *"Zeelandia, I shall impart in you all that I can. My powers, like those of all the White Queens, are unique; we don't know how they were given, or why we were chosen, but they define us — they came to us at a time when needed and helped us to fight the dark side and the forces of evil that were prevalent in our time.*

"I have been blessed with a gift from the God Androclease, who imparted in me the ability to walk amongst mystical creatures, friends of old to Arcadia, and to summon their help when needed.

"These creatures take many forms but will be by your side only whilst the spells you hold over them remain strong.

"Once summoned, your soul will be as one with theirs; you will share their pain when they feel pain, you will hurt when they feel hurt, and when they are slain the mystical spells you hold over the remainder will be weakened; a little of your soul will die alongside them.

"You must use this power wisely and know when to let them go.

"Let us begin your teaching."

Zeelandia and Arturios both picked up one of the crystal rods and sat quietly facing each other.

As she had done previously with Adelphi, both leant forwards. With their outstretched hands, they touched the remaining crystals lying on the ground before them and slowly moved the crystals they each held in each of their hands towards each other.

The crystals, as they touched, made no sound whatsoever; a light glowed from the end of each; the lights moved slowly, hovering above the ends of the rods.

A white haze wrapped itself around the bright lights and began to swirl around, and around. Gently, the beads of light moved skyward, synchronised, dancing together, hidden by the haze until they exploded into a crescendo of light and sound.

When Zeelandia had a moment to gather her thoughts, she looked up.

She was no longer in the crypt; she was standing alongside Arturios in a lush meadow. Pockets of brightly coloured flowers surrounded her and the air was filled with the most enchanting sweet smells, all around her.

Trees surrounded the spot, standing tall and to attention as though they had been planted in a giant circle to protect the area within.

Further out a deep forest of trees and vegetation was evident.

Zeelandia glanced towards Arturios, who was looking directly at Zeelandia, smiling gently in her direction.

"We are standing within the gardens of Andromonus, the spiritual home of the God Androclease, who imparted on me the great powers to walk amongst and summon the mystical beasts of this land; to be called upon only in the gravest of times.

"They have served me and Arcadia well over the centuries. Today you shall be invited to share in those powers by Androclease himself."

Zeelandia was unsure how to respond.

Arturios raised her hands above her head, closed her eyes and immediately a swirling wind enveloped her. The wind grew in intensity, swirling faster and faster. It collected blades of grass from the ground and hid Arturios from the world outside.

Slowly the wind subsided, the grass fell to the ground and Arturios had vanished.

A giant of a man stood in her place. He wore the muscly body of a Greek God; he towered over Zeelandia, who didn't flinch.

This was Androclease, the God of Andromonus.

At first there was no conversation. Androclease moved forward, turned and started to walk just beyond the tree line towards where the forest edge awaited.

He beckoned Zeelandia to follow, which she did without hesitation, and the pair disappeared into the thick forest behind.

A small path cut its way through the tree line and meandered on down a hill towards a stream.

Beside the stream a circular clearing appeared, surrounded by huge upright stones.

In the middle of the clearing two wooden staffs lay on the ground next to one another. Beside the staffs two stone thrones sat side by side.

Androclease spoke gently, *"Zeelandia, I have been asked to share with you the power I once bestowed upon Arturios many years ago.*

"This power is not to be used lightly and can only be summoned in the gravest of times.

"In years gone by, we were assisted by many who have perished for the cause. I will give you the power to call three of our greatest allies back from the dead in your times of greatest need. Use this power wisely and with great thought."

Androclease approached one of the stone thrones and sat down. Zeelandia instinctively knew that she should do the same.

The pair sat silently for a moment before Androclease lifted up one of the wooden staffs and beckoned Zeelandia to do the same, which she did without hesitation.

Androclease, holding the staff in both hands, pointed the end skyward and towards Zeelandia. He asked her to do the same and for her staff to touch his.

The two touching rods formed a bridge between the two of them. Androclease started to emit pulses of light through his body right up to the tip of his shaft.

Small cracks of sound and sparks of static electricity encircled the tips of both shafts; then suddenly and without warning, Zeelandia felt herself lift into the air; she was hovering; Androclease was hovering.

Both were holding tightly onto their shafts, which then started to rotate them round and around, slowly at first, but getting faster and faster. Zeelandia tried to hold on tight, but she couldn't change her grip; the staff had hold of her.

Spinning round and around, faster and faster, she felt herself slip into unconsciousness, and everything turned dark and silent.

When Zeelandia awoke, she was alone; it was dark, and she found herself deep within a cave system, damp and dark.

Eerie sounds filled the air, shadows flying by, light touches of something on her skin brushing by, her hair blowing. She could feel a presence all around her; she could sense movement but could see nothing at all.

As Zeelandia turned around, she could hear water dripping against rock in the distance — she followed the sound. As she made her way along the cave wall, she could see a bead of light; she headed towards it.

As she got closer, the light grew stronger and lit up a deep pool in front of her — dark and uninviting, as still as a mill pond.

Looking up, Zeelandia could see the bright blue sky high above her, peering in through a circular gap in the stone way above her head.

She sat beside the pool for a few moments, trying to regain her thoughts and make sense of the situation she now found herself in.

Zeelandia could remember her encounter with Androclease, touching staffs, spinning through the air; then nothing at all, just waking up in this strange, alien environment.

As she sat staring into the pool, suddenly and without warning, a giant head broke through the surface of the water. Attached to a long neck, the head was staring directly at her.

Scaly skin, deep grey eyes close together, pointed beak, long tongue, hissing in and out of its mouth.

Zeelandia did not flinch. She didn't move or say a word; she simply stared back at this giant water serpent now towering way above her.

This was Nadclo, a mythical water serpent, talked about in ancient scriptures, one who patrolled the water courses of the universe, protecting good from evil.

A close ally of Arcadia and an even closer friend to Arturios.

Zeelandia soon realised that Nadclo was one of the three creatures Androclease had referred to earlier, and she was sure that this meeting was no accident; it had been facilitated by Androclease, who was still conspicuous by his absence.

The large beast lowered his head and stared directly into Zeelandia's eyes. He hissed a few times, then started to speak.

"Zeelandia, please forgive my sudden appearance; the purpose was not to frighten you. These caves have been my home for many centuries. I have lain here, dormant, undisturbed, asleep. Androclease has awoken my spirit and

instructed me to serve you as you would require in your fight against the dark side.

"I am at your service; you only have to call, and I will be by your side.

"I am, as you can see, restricted to the oceans and waterways of the universe, but should you choose to take your fight along those paths, I will do all in my power to help you in your quest. That staff is your link to me. I await your instructions."

In a flash the great beast disappeared beneath the water and out of sight.

Zeelandia lifted the staff from the ground and turned around. She was unsure of what to do next. She looked up at the sky above her head and decided to climb the wall of the cave towards the light and fresh air high above her head.

The rocks were loose, but there were enough firm hand holds to see her safely to the top.

She climbed out of the hole and found herself on top of a hillside. As she scanned the horizon, rolling hills spread out before her as far as she could see. The air was still, clear and silent.

Zeelandia sat down on the grass. She lay the staff beside her and began to gather her thoughts once again.

As she listened, she heard a quiet whirring noise above her head and looked up.

A giant butterfly hovered above her head, translucent wings with silver tips, ten or twelve of them along each wing, long and protruding like giant daggers.

This was Vonarx, another ally that Zeelandia could call on — this serene creature was not all that she appeared to be.

Her giant wings were impenetrable. No spear, dagger, axe or any dragon's breath could penetrate her shield. In battle those silver tips became deadly weapons.

Vonarx bowed her head. *"Zeelandia, I am here to serve you; use the staff to call me if you need my help, and I will be by your side in an instant."* Her wings flapped together, she rose high above the clouds overhead and vanished out of sight in an instant.

Zeelandia could hear a faint rumbling in the distance; she turned around and saw a cloud of dust rising from the ground way out in the horizon, far ahead.

The rumbling got louder and louder and the churning dust ball got closer and closer.

An army of Adronolites stood before her, each one to attention.

Adronolites formed the personal army of Androclease. They were half man and half buffalo.

A man's body, giant, muscular in stature with large muscular arms, with a huge buffalo's head on the top of a wide neck; black, menacing, with great dagger-like horns on top of their heads. Rings through their noses, snorting for breath.

Mohtah, the leader of this great army, knelt before Zeelandia, put his right hand across his chest, his fist clasped tightly shut. *"Androclease has bestowed upon me and my men the honour of standing by your side in battle. We will await your instructions, my queen."*

Then, as fast as they had arrived, the army of soldiers disappeared.

Zeelandia was struggling to take all of this in and looked up to the sky for guidance. She closed her eyes, reopened them once more and found herself back in the crypt of Arcadia. Sitting on a glass chair — all alone.

Adelphi walked into the room and sat down beside her.

She held her hand and whispered gently across to her:

"That is your first teaching, Zeelandia, and although you have travelled well, we must make haste with the rest of your teachings.

"Vandermortel, as we speak, has reached the grasslands of Citronus, and the battle for that kingdom is about to take place.

"You cannot fully influence the outcome from here, but you can witness the battle from within these walls — at best your spirit may have some small part to play, but until you leave this place you can have little active part to play.

"Tomorrow we must prepare you ready for further teaching, and we must get you back to the mortal land to assist with this great fight as soon as we possibly can."

Zeelandia withdrew her hand from her mother's grasp, arose from the chair and walked out of the crypt into an adjacent chamber.

In the stark, empty room, a single wooden chair stood in the middle of the room. Beside the chair a wooden table resting on three legs wore the heavy burden of an opaque glass ball sitting upon it.

Zeelandia walked over to the chair and sat down facing the glass ball.

She placed both hands on the ball and began to speak: *"timra, saloni, soosha, atogah, jesta, timra, saloni, soosha, atogah, jesta, timra, saloni, soosha, atogah, jesta."* She repeated the phrase over and over again, ten, possibly twenty times. Slowly the ball started to bring into focus a picture from within.

She could see Vandermortel, Solway, Galphia, Jeerplah and Degla holding council.

Behind them, she could see tens of thousands of dark riders, dismounted from their horses and standing to attention, dark cloaks hiding their grotesque faces, swords and daggers already drawn, ready and eager for battle.

The picture rotated, and she found herself looking towards the opposite end of the battlefield to be.

Xanti, Astrolis, Trevelous and Insignia were sat round an open fire. Xanti was holding a wooden stick in his right hand and was marking the ground with what looked to be a battle plan.

Row upon row of dwarfs filled the landscape as far as the eye could see, stretching way up the valley before them. They too were prepared for battle.

Zeelandia took a deep breath, she closed her eyes for a few seconds to regain her focus and again turned to the glass ball and the story it was about to tell.

The Battle for Citronus

Galphia and Degla stepped back from their master, bowed their heads, flapped their giant wings and rose above Vandermortel's head, hovering just above him and facing down the valley towards Citronus.

Vandermortel had Solway by his right-hand side, with Jeerplah directly in front of his master. Any dwarf would have to get past him if they wished to have a direct encounter with Vandermortel.

Vandermortel turned to his dark riders and gave the command to attack.

The marauding hordes led by Vandermortel, Solway and Jeerplah ran down the valley, closing in fast on the dwarf army ahead, with every stride picking up speed. Faster and faster they ran until there were but a few feet between them.

Xanti and his allies had already taken up their positions at the front of the assembled Citronic army, anticipating the moment of conflict.

Xanti gave the command, the front twenty rows knelt down and the archers were given free rein to unleash a barrage of arrows and spears skyward towards Vandermortel's advancing army.

Hundreds of dark riders were slain and fell to the ground, unable to avoid the tirade of arrowheads set loose upon them. But it made little dent to the colossal army following behind.

The first twenty rows of dwarfs and their defence stood firm, resolute, large spears wedged into the ground behind them, pointing upwards and towards the fast advancing enemy.

Jeerplah was the first to break through the well-drilled defence, this giant rhino with almost impenetrable skin; three huge tusked heads made light work of the tiny dwarfs, the first protectors of Citronus.

He sliced through them with little resistance, tossing them high into the air, impaling them on his giant tusks. Galphia swooped down from the sky and fought by his master's side. Degla flew overhead, deep into the defending army, picking off his victims, snapping them between his sharp jaws and tossing them back to the ground from high above the battlefield.

Soon the dwarfs' first defences were overrun, and the battle for the grasslands had truly began.

Swords drawn, daggers at the ready, axes slicing throughout the air, shields used to defend, dwarf after dwarf and dark rider after dark rider fell to the ground, with injuries inflicted so gruesome, but each and every one proving fatal in one way or another.

Heads decapitated, limbs ripped off, wounds to torsos as swords and daggers sliced through the flesh and bone of both armies.

Barbaric, primeval, basic instincts displayed, a need, will and determination to survive on both sides — brutal and unforgiving.

This carnage continued from first light, closing in on sunset, when Vandermortel finally signalled his troops back up the valley to regroup and prepare for the battle he would re-commence at first light.

The casualties were great on both sides; however, it had taken a greater toll on the dwarfs of Citronus, who were very close to being completely decimated on this first day alone. Their numbers had been heavily depleted.

Xanti, his close allies and his people above all had fought like true warriors this day, but they knew sunrise would probably be a challenge too far, given the scale of losses Xanti had endured this day.

Xanti, Astrolis, Trevelous and Insignia had all drawn their fair share of blood that day. They headed back to the entrance to the Caves of Citronus to discuss their options — options that were truly few indeed.

As they stared into the fire, one flickering flame stood out.

It turned from red to orange and then blue.

As it danced above the flames surrounding it, a figure appeared — it was that of Zeelandia. The figure rotated, slowly: a mystical figure in a long white dress, she spoke quietly.

"There is little I can do to help you in this battle, but I have summoned the help of the Adronolites who will stand beside you in battle tomorrow. They will be few in number, but nonetheless they will do what they can. They will attack Vandermortel from behind as he marches towards your

position — hopefully this distraction will assist you." The flame fell back into formation, and Zeelandia was gone.

The four lords discussed at length their strategy for the next day — they would fight on and await assistance from the Adronolites, then on command fall back into the caves as agreed and take this battle to Vandermortel on their own terms, not his.

Xanti had already fortified the caves, with men strategically placed, ready to ambush the attacking army when signalled to do so.

The night was long, dark and cold; in the distance fires were raging, dark riders were feasting on their own dead; Vandermortel and his allies were contemplating their next move.

"We will strike at first light," Vandermortel spoke calmly. *"We have them on the back foot and we outnumber them ten to one — tomorrow will be our victory and we will move one kingdom closer to my freedom.*

"Xanti and the Citronic people will be wiped out; we shall return and claim the spoils of this land when we have completed our crusade."

The night rolled on and the dawn soon arrived.

Xanti set his men up as before and hoped and prayed that this day would end better than he in his heart knew it would.

Vandermortel's army advanced once again at pace, and leading the charge was Jeerplah; no one expected a different outcome to the last — Jeerplah charging through the meagre battle line that had been drawn — unopposed, unstoppable.

Then suddenly and without warning, ten Adronolites appeared as though summoned from the earth below, led by Mohtah. Their huge buffalo heads locked and united; in unison they charged directly towards Jeerplah, as one giant buffalo standing as one beast together — the collision sent a shuddering wave through the landscape. Jeerplah was knocked to the ground and rolled over, the Adronolites surrounded the massive beast and charged, and charged at him, again and again, hitting him from all angles, knocking him to the ground, again and again.

Jeerplah lifted himself up and charged at his opponents; one by one he slayed them until only Mohtah stood in his way.

It would have taken one hundred Adronolites, not ten, to get the better of this giant beast. Mohtah put up a fierce and ferocious fight against this giant beast probably ten times his size, but in the end Jeerplah prevailed and drove his longest and sharpest tusk straight through Mohtah's heart.

Jeerplah had not come out of this battle unscathed. He bore heavy scars across each of his three heads and had lost two eyes against the warrior that was Mohtah.

Instantaneously a battalion of five hundred Adronolites appeared to the rear of Vandermortel's army and began their attack, cutting down dark rider after dark rider.

The dwarfs, sensing this surge of power, fought with a renewed vigour.

The battle raged on until Xanti finally sounded the retreat. From the rear of the battlefield the dwarfs, obeying their lord's signal, retreated deep into the caves.

Xanti and the three other lords saw the last of Xanti's men enter the caves before following on behind themselves; the Adronolites had bought them enough time to choreograph this retreat whilst they distracted Vandermortel and his grotesque army.

The grasslands fell silent; the last of the Adronolites had sacrificed themselves and fallen. Vandermortel's attention was now focused on the battle within the caves that would follow.

Vandermortel instructed Galphia and Degla to take to the air and make their way to the south of the Citronus range and await his emergence from the caves when the final battle was won.

"You are of little use to me here. Make safe the cave exit and wait for me there."

The pair did not even stop to question their master's instructions — they turned around, flapped their giant wings and rose high into the sky and out of sight.

Xanti held his last council with his three comrades — they all stood facing each other, each put out their right hands and they each clasped each other's fists.

"My comrades, your battle here is over. Make your way through my mountains and prepare for your next battle — it will be upon you sooner than you think.

"We will do all that we can to hinder Vandermortel's progress, but we cannot stop him.

"Astrolis, you are the next to stand in his way — may God be with you, my friend.

"I hope one day we will all be reunited — in better circumstances."

The three did as they were asked and headed off through the maze of mountain tunnels under the guidance of a young dwarf.

The labyrinth of caves filled the mountain, and they lay silent. Vandermortel, Solway and Jeerplah quickly reached the entrance to the cave's intricate system.

Tens of thousands of dark riders covered the grasslands as far as the eye could see.

For all that a heavy battle had ensued, and the losses heavy, the dark riders just kept coming and coming, their presence and their numbers relentless.

Xanti made his way through the cave system and headed to the west side where five hundred men were waiting for him as instructed.

This place would give them the greatest opportunity to ambush Vandermortel and drive him towards the great hall on the east side where Xanti's two brothers and son were waiting to take up the fight as planned.

As he arrived, the troops were assembled as requested, and a great cheer filled the air as their lord and king joined them.

They waited and waited; a sound of thunder could be heard in the distance. The caves were shaking, as though hit by one explosion, then another, then another.

Back at the cave entrance the source of this great disturbance was evident.

Jeerplah was using his great size and might to charge his way through the small tunnels, enlarging them and making it easy for Vandermortel and his men to pass.

The advantage no longer lay with the people of Citronus; this was now a battle just like any other.

As Vandermortel's army progressed through the mountain range, other side tunnels joined, and it was at these points that dwarfs in their hundreds lay ambush and fought valiantly in an effort to deplete Vandermortel's vast numbers and delay his progress.

Xanti could hear the battle getting closer and closer to his position and, in no time at all, he and his brave five hundred found themselves at the heart of the battle.

They drove the marauding dark riders back and eastward, but still Vandermortel progressed.

All within the Great Hall could hear the deafening shouts and screams outside: swords smashing against shields, death and destruction, carnage just a few feet away from them. They could hear Xanti, shouting orders to his men.

Theagor ran towards the two huge oak doors, the only thing separating them from the battle outside.

Tryson stood in front of him. *"We must stay as instructed until the fighting passes by. That is your father's order."*

"No!" shouted Theagor. *"We must go now and stand shoulder to shoulder with the king."*

"I hear what you are saying, and I want more than anything to open those doors — but your father and Citronus will not thank us if we do."

Sharjay was sitting quietly. He interjected: *"Five more minutes and we will engage. Patience, dear boy, patience."*

The commotion quickly died down, Tryson gave the order to open the great doors and they charged out, chasing down the dark riders in their sights.

Xanti was there right at the heart of the battle, soon joined by his two brothers and his son, fighting side by side.

As they made their way through the caverns, a spear bolted out from a cave to the left and hit Sharjay, piercing his armour and embedding itself deep in his chest.

The scream let out by Xanti filled the air. He turned to see a dark rider hiding in the shadows, he lunged at the despicable creature and drove his sword through the creature's chest and out the other side. As he pulled his sword out and as the creature fell to its knees, Xanti with one final motion decapitated the pathetic beast and left it to fall uncontrollably to the ground.

Xanti rushed to his brother's side. Sharjay, cradled by Xanti, lay quietly on the ground, blood pouring from the edge of the gaping wound that still gripped the spear deep inside his body.

A few moments later, Sharjay was gone.

This final conflict ensued well into the night; bodies were strewn all around; casualties were again heavy on both sides.

Xanti, Tryson and Theagor fought like no other mortal had ever fought before, revenging the death of their beloved brother and uncle.

Jeerplah made his last charge, and as the rocks crumbled before him, the valley to the south of the Citronus range appeared before them.

This savage dark army had safely navigated Citronus and the first kingdom had failed to stop them; the battle of Citronus was over, and Vandermortel was one step closer to freedom.

As morning arrived, Sharjay's body was recovered and taken to a place deep within the mountain range. Xanti turned. Theagor stood by his side. *"Where is Tryson?"* Xanti asked.

"I don't know, father, I haven't seen him since we returned to the mountain."

One dwarf shouted: *"He headed out of the mountain at first light. I haven't seen him since."*

Xanti knew this was not good news. Tryson had been distraught at the death of his brother; Xanti had calmed him down the night before when he was set on revenge — Xanti in his heart felt that Tryson had not left the battle behind.

"Stay with the men, Theagor, I will search for your uncle." At that Xanti ran off through the mountain tunnel and out of sight before Theagor could even raise a question.

Tryson could see a group of dark riders huddled together, close to a sheer rock face. A fire was raging and thick black smoke coiled skyward from the flames.

A pungent smell filled the air, the smell of burning flesh, repugnant, putrid.

On the fire several dwarf bodies were piled, two rotating on a spit, each burning slowly in the intense heat. Almost ready to be eaten.

Tryson wasted no time in engaging with the dark riders slaying each before they had time to even draw their swords.

He dragged each of the bodies from the fire and laid them to rest on the ground beside him, dousing the flames as he did so.

He was unaware of the trap that had been set for him. He heard a noise from above, looked up to see a heavy, thick chain net envelop him, the weight of which pulled him to the ground, trapping him underneath, and rendered him helpless to fight back.

He was immediately surrounded by dark riders, hissing and spitting, salivating from their mouths and long pointed noses.

They kicked and punched him, clubbed him with large wooden sticks and beat him back to the ground each and every time he tried to get up.

Eventually Tryson had no fight left and felt the sharp pain as a sword was driven into his back. He could hear the dark riders laughing and screaming, desperate for the blood of one more dwarf.

One of them stood over Tryson and pulled the net away. He lifted his sword high into the air, and just as he was about to drive it into Tryson, Tryson could see his father Valert standing beside him. Valert turned to Tryson, who summoned up inner strength from where he knew not, picked up his sword and the two fought one last battle together.

The odds were stacked against them, hundreds of dark riders came at them, one, then another, then another; the two dwarfs, fighting valiantly side by side, did all that they could to reduce their numbers. Valert disappeared; Tryson was alone, on his knees, two dark riders holding him down and another with a sword to his neck.

As the blade prepared to make its final cut, Vandermortel intervened. He bellowed: *"Solway, bring that dwarf to me."* Vandermortel was high above the ground at the top of the sheer rock face. Solway jumped down, pushed the dark riders out of the way and grabbed the dwarf.

He dragged Tryson up the mountain to his master and threw him down at his master's feet.

"Ha, Ha, Ha, look what we have here, I believe it's Tryson, the brother of the Dwarf King Xanti. My Gelopodites killed your father, and I'm sure before this day is out both you and the mighty Xanti will see him again — in hell. Gag him and string him up."

Tryson was bound and gagged and hung from the branch of an old cedar tree high up on the hillside, in clear view of the path below, but with enough protection to hide the waiting Vandermortel, Solway and a number of dark riders.

As expected, Xanti appeared. He could see the smouldering embers of a fire, and at least one hundred dark riders, slain, their bodies covering the ground in front of him — he knew this was Tryson's doing.

His eye was drawn to the skyline above his head. He immediately saw the figure of his brother swinging slowly in the wind, hanging from the tree; he could see he was still alive.

At that Theagor arrived with one hundred men and stood beside Xanti. *"Father, you know this is a trap."*

"Yes, I do, son, but I cannot let my brother down. If he dies this day, then I will die trying to save him. He will not die alone."

"Then we will all die this day, father."

"No, my son. Citronus needs a king, and that king will be you."

The pair argued, but from Theagor's perspective, to no avail — Xanti, with the butt of his sword, hit Theagor across the face, knocking him to the ground, where he lay unconscious, but not seriously hurt. Xanti ordered twenty of the men to stand guard over him and made them swear they would keep Theagor from the fight.

Xanti asked for volunteers; they were not short in coming forward. *"This will be our last battle, if you choose to fight with me. Today we will no doubt meet our maker, but you shall not die in vain — you will be legends within Citronus for all eternity."*

They raised their swords and charged up the mountainside, led by Xanti.

Dark rider after dark rider stood in their way as they made their way towards Tryson.

One by one dark rider after dark rider fell to the ground, followed by the culling of the brave dwarfs.

Xanti approached the top of the hillside and could see Vandermortel and Solway standing beside his brother. Solway slashed his sword and sliced through the rope suspending Tryson from the tree.

He fell heavily to the ground and was immediately lifted by his hair to his knees.

Solway pulled his dagger from its sheath and slit Tryson's throat. Blood gushed from the gaping wound, and the dwarf slumped to the ground. Solway roared with laughter. *"Come on, mighty Dwarf King — join your week and feeble brother as he burns in hell."*

For Xanti the world moved in slow motion: he found himself charging towards Solway, sword in hand; he looked to his right, and by his side was his father, Valert, running beside him.

He could see his brother's spirit rising from the ground. He hadn't even noticed the fatal blow that had been rained down upon him.

A tirade of arrows had been unleashed upon him and struck him in a thousand places at once. His very existence was extinguished in an instant.

Xanti stood upright with his father standing proud beside him; joined by Tryson, the father and two sons, reunited for one final time in battle, faded away into eternity.

Vandermortel turned to Solway, *"Let us be on our way and prepare to do battle with the Dragon Master."*

They turned, mounted their horses and sped off into the distance, leaving a trail of dust in their wake.

Theagor opened his eyes, still groggy from the blow to his head.

He looked up and was helped to his feet by one of the dwarfs. *"Where is my father?"* he asked. They gestured to the top of the mountain.

Theagor drew his sword and raced up the steep slopes, but all too late.

On reaching the top he could see two figures lying on the ground close to the base of an old cedar tree. He knew instantly who they were.

He walked over to them and threw his body down on the ground beside them and held them close.

The leaves were rustling gently in the wind; the skies were clear and blue; the air was hot and still.

Theagor looked up and could see a small multi-coloured butterfly dancing between the leaves, its reds, yellows and blues flickering in the bright sunlight. It started to spin round and round, falling slowly to the ground.

The delicate creature landed gently beside Theagor and immediately started to change its form. It was cocooned in a whirlwind of dust, which spun faster and faster, moving slowly skyward. Then, in front of Theagor, it changed its outward appearance completely, and standing there in front of him was an image of Zeelandia.

She was standing inside a crystal vessel, with him, but still a million miles away. She was there in spirit but not in body.

Zeelandia spoke gently. *"My dear Theagor, your father and brothers have made the ultimate sacrifice for Citronus, Arcadia and indeed for freedom and for good itself.*

"They will never be forgotten. Your people have done all that you can for now — take your father and uncles and lay them to rest.

"For now, your fight is over. You are now the King of Citronus — wear your crown well, my friend, and if the Gods will be on our side, one day we will meet again."

As quickly as she had appeared, Zeelandia was gone. Theagor did as he was asked.

Further Secrets of the White Queens Revealed

Once again Zeelandia entered the crypt and took up her position in the glass chair adjacent to the column of crystal rods, directly in front of the second glass chair again standing empty opposite her, just as she had done previously whilst sitting with Adelphi, and then Arturios.

Sherideso walked into the crypt and took up her position in the chair opposite Zeelandia.

She was petite in stature, with deep green eyes and long flowing jet-black hair tied tightly to the back.

She, like all of the White Queens, wore a stunning long white dress, very plain but nonetheless equally breathtaking as any Zeelandia had seen before.

A delicate tiara encrusted with deep red rubies adorned her head, sitting perfectly, the colours glistening and bringing a stark contrast and perspective between her dark hair and white dress she wore so beautifully.

They each picked up one of the crystal rods and sat quietly facing each other.

As they leant forward, with their outstretched hands they touched the remaining crystals lying on the ground before them and slowly moved the crystals they each held in each of their hands towards one another.

The crystals, as they touched, again made no sound whatsoever; a light glowed from the end of each. The lights moved slowly, hovering above the ends of the rods.

A white haze wrapped itself around the bright lights and began to swirl around, and around. Gently the beads of light moved skyward, synchronised, dancing together, hidden by the haze until they exploded into a crescendo of light and sound, bright and deafening.

Zeelandia found herself flying through the air, then without warning, plunged into complete darkness.

She was spinning uncontrollably towards the ground but had no sense of where she was or what was happening to her. The spinning eventually slowed down, and she felt the force of gravity on her body directing her feet carefully to the solid ground below.

As she regained a sense of her surroundings, she found herself standing next to Sherideso.

The atmosphere was hot and smelled strongly of sulphur. Molten lava surrounded them both, bubbling, spitting, a cauldron of flames all around.

Sherideso turned to Zeelandia. *"Do not be afraid. Take my hand and follow me."* Zeelandia did this without hesitation. They walked towards the flames and the molten lava, then walked straight on, directly into the inferno itself, allowing themselves to be engulfed.

There was no sensation of burning, no heat, no intensity; it was just peaceful, tranquil, surreal.

Then without warning, Zeelandia found herself caught up in the inferno. The flames enveloped her, swirling her around and around, causing her body to spin faster and faster.

The flames flickered around her; she saw flames and fire all around. Everything entered slow motion. She could see right into the eye of some deep red molten precipice — she was transported right to its edge and pulled back again, again and again and again- then all became calm; the flames gently extinguished and died down around her. Zeelandia stopped spinning, and the pair walked forward together, still hand in hand.

Sherideso broke the silence. *"This is the source of all fire, and you have been granted the power to call upon this immense force of nature, just as it was passed to me in times gone by — use this power with great care, my child."*

The pair walked down a path of hard, dark volcanic rock and ash, carved out from the mountainside by some lava flow centuries before. There was no sense of the intense heat which they had left behind on this branded landscape.

The path was long and winding, and after several minutes the pair ended up at a small open chamber.

Zeelandia could hear in the distance a faint whining noise, like a gentle breeze snaking its way past the rock face and caressing a steep cliff, seeking out every crevasse and undulation it may happen upon.

The noise grew louder and louder until it turned into a crescendo of unbearable sound. Zeelandia placed her hands over her ears to try to deaden the sound, but it just kept coming, louder and louder.

Suddenly and without warning, a tornado manifested itself in front of her, picking her up like a rag doll and spinning her around and around, lifting her higher and higher, out of the mountain and taking her on a violent journey, rolling quickly over a deep green field beyond. Uprooting trees and buildings as it sped on and on, picking up speed and intensity as it did so.

It passed over land to the sea, pulled oceans of water skyward and then dispersed it back on to the land without concern for the destruction its actions may have.

The power of the tornado diminished in intensity. Zeelandia felt herself slowing down within the grasp of this mighty storm.

Gently it placed her back on solid ground, standing high up on a hillside. Trees were strewn all around, gullies were cut through the earth, long furrows as though fashioned by some enormous plough, dancing out of control.

Sherideso was once again standing by Zeelandia's side. *"The power of the wind is now yours,"* she uttered.

Before Zeelandia had time to respond, Sherideso beckoned her to look skyward.

As she did so, she saw a bolt of lightning rush from the sky. It struck her with such intensity, knocking her deep into the ground, then instantaneously picking her up and levitating her just above the earth below.

Beads of light danced around her body, emitted from every part of her writhing frame, pulsating, searching, prying. This electric show lasted for moments, cocooning her body with the intensity of its very being. Again, gently she was placed on the ground and this dazzling expression of power receded.

Zeelandia awoke to find herself sitting once again on one of the glass chairs within the crypt. The other was empty; she was all alone.

A few seconds passed by as she regained her thoughts. Then Adelphi walked into the crypt and sat on the chair opposite her.

"My darling Zeelandia, your time with Sherideso is over, and she has shared with you what she can. You now have the power to summon the forces of nature — Fire, Wind and Lightning.

"You still have a lot to learn, but you will only leave this crypt to do so one more time.

"You will travel with Heathrodece and take on her teachings, but before then you will spend time with Flymoro. She has no specific powers, but is one of Arcadia's greatest White Queens. She will impart to you great powers of sorcery that will serve you well.

"Many of these powers you will be unaware of. They will lie dormant within your soul, waiting to be called.

"Your final teaching, before transcending back to the mortal world, will be spent with me, where I will share with you Arcadia's history and the battles of the past, hopefully passing on lessons learned.

"For now, my child, take some rest, as Vandermortel prepares his mighty army to do battle with Astrolis in the Land of Dragons."

Adelphi arose from the chair and left the crypt. Zeelandia followed closely behind and headed off to the resting chamber, but, instead of resting, decided to consult the crystal ball of destiny, searching for the mortal world and what was happening in that land.

The Land of Dragons

Astrolis, Trevelous and Insignia sat round a raging fire deliberating and pondering the battle for Citronus and the fate of their dear friends and comrades Tryson, Sharjay and not least Xanti, who had all given their lives for the cause.

Astrolis raised his glass and proposed a toast to the trio and to the hundreds of brave dwarfs who had fought so valiantly in that great battle.

Their focus could not dwell on the past for too long, as they needed to agree the strategy for the battle to come.

Trevelous and Insignia would be of little use here, as only Astrolis and his people could command the great dragon army within his lands.

As they spoke, the bright reds and oranges of the fire turned to blue as though starved of oxygen; the flames grew weaker and weaker, eventually extinguishing. From the smouldering embers a light swirling wind of ash rose, rotating round and around, growing in size and power.

The ash mist dissipated and left behind the figure of Zeelandia, encased within a glass dome, standing directly in front of them.

"My lords, it is with a heavy heart indeed that I have learned of the fall of Citronus and the fate of Tryson, Sharjay and Xanti, along with many of their people.

"Theagor has taken up his place as the new and rightful King of Citronus now; his people are in good hands.

"I am unable to transcend back to your mortal world at this time, but I will continue to do all that I can to support you in this battle ahead from afar, until at last I can be by your side in battle."

As quickly as she had arrived, Zeelandia faded back into the glowing embers of the extinguished fire, immediately re-igniting it and sending the flames dancing skyward once again, bringing heat and comfort to the surroundings.

The three comrades fell silent for a moment, reflecting, contemplating, then quickly refocused on the battle to come, this time reassured that they had not just Zeelandia but the might of Arcadia and its White Queens alongside them. All was not lost.

As instructed, Degla and Galphia waited at the exit to the caves of Citronus, where Jeerplah, followed by Vandermortel, Solway and the dark riders emerged, victorious after their battle through the mountain ranges.

They had stood by and watched as Solway despatched Tryson, and then Xanti met his end under that tirade of arrows. There was no more work to be done here.

Vandermortel pulled together his allies to discuss the pending battle in Verow, the Land of Dragons.

It would take them three days and three nights to reach Astrolis's Kingdom, and there would be no rest for his men until they had reached their next point of conflict.

A dark shadow was cast heavy over the entire landscape, reaching far across the land and indeed throughout the universe.

Vandermortel's strength was growing day by day, his power and presence was on the rise, ever stronger; the universe could feel the heavy weight of dread and fear growing all around.

Vandermortel, encircled by Solway, Jeerplah, Degla and Galphia, rose to his feet, his four allies surrounding him.

They were standing on a gentle grassy slope high above the Citronus ranges and the clear blue skies, cloudless, unblemished, spread out far and wide around them.

Vandermortel raised his hands, elevating them high above his head, standing tall in the egrath's body. He closed his eyes, and the clear blue skies darkened in an instant.

The spirits of the dark side were summoned, and the dark clouds circled all around on his command.

This was Vandermortel's world, and both he and it grew stronger with every day that passed.

He pulled in the power of the dark, ravenous for the intake of strength and the supremacy it bestowed upon him. This indulgence lasted for hours. Vandermortel was recharging, re-energising after that first battle; he would be stronger and harder to stop with every hour that now passed.

Morning arrived, though it was hard to determine night from day as the darkness spread. The only glimmer of light evident was as the Land of Verow appeared in the distance.

Vandermortel and his army were on the march and would not rest until they had reached the battlefield to come.

Astrolis walked amongst his men. It was his turn to hold council, yet he knew not what to say at that point.

They had three days and nights to prepare, but for what — a battle, that was inevitable, but how, where, when and to what end?

Astrolis had three generals by his side: Kane, Trellis and Slate, each great warriors in their own right and great dragon masters within their lands.

The three had arrived earlier that day, carried by their trusty steeds — three of the mightiest dragons ever seen within the Land of Dragons.

The generals had not chosen their dragons — the dragons chose them at birth; they were raised by the dragons within the Kingdom — of Verow. That was the way of this land.

Dragons roamed free — they were in charge; they would choose their dragon masters to be, when they were but infants.

The dragons would patrol the night sky, looking for their match, and when they felt a connection, would swoop from the sky and carry off their prey.

The infants were taken high up into the mountain ranges and placed in great nests made out of vines and thick branches from trees, bent and twisted by the hot, fiery breath of these mystical beasts.

The infants would be fed raw flesh from prey stalked and killed, brought back to the nest for feeding, and when old enough, would be taught the ways of the dragon.

From that moment on the pair would be inseparable; only death would tear them apart. Dragon masters took control of this partnership, when and only when they had reached a rite of passage and the challenges and rituals associated with such a rite were successfully completed.

As far as the eye could see, dragon after dragon waited, their masters dismounted, standing to attention, awaiting instruction from Astrolis and his generals.

They all knew the gravity of the situation, what would be asked of them and the sacrifices already made by the people of Citronus. These dragon masters were not ones to shirk a fight, however bloody, or however unlikely success would be.

As Vandermortel closed in on this land, the skies around it darkened further; the power of the dark side was taking hold and starting to exert a grip on Verow, even before any battle had taken place.

It was undeniably worrying times for all who inhabited this land and indeed the universe as a whole — the dark shadow spread far and wide and brought with it a still, stagnant chill to the air that had not been felt for a long time.

Vandermortel's great army marched on, night and day. They needed no rest, they took none; passing grasslands, mountain ranges, coming to rest eventually on the banks of the great lake to the north of Verow and the Land of Dragons, awaiting their signal from Vandermortel — when and where to attack.

As the dark riders sat, squabbled and fought on the bank of the great lake, Vandermortel walked quietly amongst them, the despicable creatures that made up this vast army, hideous and a mirror image of hell itself, visible for all to see.

They happily fought each other, hunger driving cannibalistic behaviours, slaughtering their own injured, tearing flesh from their bones and eating raw skin, sinew and muscle: a feeding frenzy of hunger driving deeds and actions reserved only for the purest of evil itself.

Zeelandia was watching from afar, unable to do anything but perhaps offer a pre-battle distraction.

Looking into the ball of destiny, she summoned up Nadclo to assist. The hideous army to start with didn't even notice the arrival of Nadclo — the giant water serpent moved with ease along the shallow waters to the edge of the great lake, picking off dark rider after dark rider.

Scooping them up in his great jaws, slicing through their flesh and tossing them deep into the lake towards the bottomless dark, cold waters and abyss that stretched out far below the surface.

Nadclo buried himself deep underground, burrowing great tunnels, driving through the solid ground far inland and dragging his enemy far out of sight, back to the lake.

The army turned and fought back, but they knew not where he would strike next.

The ground would shake violently and open up, Nadclo would grab ten dark riders at a time, then disappear in an instant. Returning soon after, surprising the great army who could not anticipate where he would strike next.

Galphia, the great winged lion, was the first to react. He soared high into the sky, circling way above the commotion unfolding below. He watched; he studied the pattern of attacks develop far beneath him, looking to anticipate Nadclo's next move.

The great lion could see the underground furrows appear; he could see where Nadclo would present himself next, but each and every time, just as he swooped down, ready to strike as the giant serpent broke through the surface, he was just too late.

Time after time Nadclo broke through the surface, disrupting the great army, which was powerless to fight back.

Vandermortel's army was in disarray, stabbing at the ground in every direction, looking to strike out at a foe who could not be seen.

Galphia saw his chance. He swooped in from the east and followed a line of vibrations along the lake surface; the ripples on the water disappeared as Nadclo left the water course and headed inland. This time, as Nadclo broke through the surface, Galphia was waiting.

His huge frame came flying down from the sky and wrapping his immense jaws around Nadclo's neck, gripping on and biting it with all his might.

Nadclo shook his head violently from side to side, trying to dislodge Galphia's grip, but to no avail. His body was being dragged by the colossal power of Galphia high above the ground, writhing, snaking round, but Galphia's grip was not loosening — he gripped even tighter, and tighter, driving his long, jagged teeth deeper into Nadclo's neck.

Nadclo would not allow himself to be torn free from the tunnel below. Hanging on by the end of his tail, he gripped for dear life.

He could feel his skin deflect the swords and spears rained down upon it by the thousands of dark riders surrounding him, none strong enough to break through his thick scales.

Momentarily he stopped resisting; then, in one final movement, he pulled Galphia groundward, and into the tunnel he had just created and appeared from a few moments before.

Both disappeared below the surface and out of view. The ground shook violently below the surface as the pair fought ruthlessly underground; it then fell calm as Nadclo pulled

Galphia deep into the lake and the murky bottomless waters filling it.

All was silent — Degla took to the skies, looking for any sign of Galphia or indeed a sign of life in any form, any movement, any struggle; all that could be seen were tiny bubbles rising from deep beneath the surface of the shadowy, soulless waters far below.

No sign of either Nadclo or Galphia — both engrossed in their struggle, falling weightlessly through the water towards the centre of the earth and down into the abyss below.

This was a blow to Vandermortel. Galphia, with his great power and ability to fly, would have had an important role to play in the battle for the skies in the Land of Dragons. But there was no time for sentiment. He was gone.

Both sides reflected on their losses, but their attention swiftly moved to the battle ahead.

Astrolis sat with his three generals — Kane, Trellis and Slate. In years gone by, they had each been chosen by their dragons at the same time; they had all been abducted from the same village on the same night.

For years they spent their time high up on the same mountainside, higher than any other dragons dared to go — the nests they occupied were adjacent to one another, precariously perched, overhanging the sheer cliff face and the five thousand feet drop below.

They were not ones for sitting idly in their nests; they could often be found traversing the sheer rock face and spending time in each other's company, inquisitive, fearless, inventive and resourceful.

Their dragons would often be away for days at a time — these three young generals occupied their time imaginatively, working out strategies to fill their long days, even at that young age.

The trio grew up in separation from the thousands of dragons and dragon masters who inhabited this stark landscape; no other would venture this high up.

A lush velvet carpet of grass sat at the top of the mountain peak, snow-covered in winter, but as baking hot as the sun itself in summer.

A dense woodland roamed across this grassland and provided food and shelter for the many animals the dragons and the dragon masters would feed upon.

Deep crystal-clear pools of water interrupted the scenery, teeming with life and undisturbed in this mountain hideaway, unknown to the outside world.

Little did they know, as they grew up in isolation and learned their trade, that their destiny would unfold before them in the days to come.

The great lake swallowed up the landscape, the shoreline to the east, where Vandermortel and his army sat, the only solid ground for a hundred miles. The vast waterway meandered around vast rocks driven skyward centuries ago by enormous volcanic eruptions, creating a jagged range of impenetrable mountains peeping out of the shadowy water far below.

To the west of this location sat a tranquil valley, out of sight, hidden from the prying world, invisible to outsiders.

This land was the source of dragon masters. Villages littered the landscape, farmers, fishermen — simple people.

All worshipped the Gods of the sky: the Dragons. Dragons had looked after this land for centuries and in return asked only to choose their dragon masters.

The people of this land considered it an honour to offer this simple sacrifice — one which had kept them safe and protected throughout time.

Dragons patrolled the night sky, protecting, engaging and fending off intruders who dared wander into this stark landscape.

Traders, thieves, bandits, all intent on stealing the rich abundance of precious stones buried deep within the mountain ranges, hidden from view, but of whom stories and myths brought many people in search of their riches.

It was at this place Astrolis and his generals amassed their great dragon army, waiting to be called into action.

The vast numbers of dragons and dragon masters covered the landscape as far as the eye could see — awaiting their command to attack.

Vandermortel summoned Degla. The giant reptile knelt before his master, and his master mounted him, sitting astride his neck. *"Take me to Waldron,"* he commanded.

The immense reptile flapped his giant wings, and the pair rose quickly into the evening sky, quickly rising high above the clouds, picking up speed, faster and faster, through the atmosphere, through space and time.

Stars, comets, meteorites passed them by — time stood still, but still they travelled on through the vastness of space.

Waldron was dark and desolate, lifeless, serrated rock structures pointing high into the sky. Dry, barren. Heavy shadows were cast across the gaps between the rocky peaks, and an eerie whistling wind spiralled all around.

Degla approached an outcrop, a platform fashioned from the rock itself, hanging suspended against a backdrop of a hundred stone pillars, each standing upright and giving shape and substance to the level area they now stood on.

Vandermortel dismounted and walked to the centre of the arena. Degla made his way to the rear of the platform close to the sheer rock face stretching hundreds of feet high above, away from Vandermortel but still within his master's view.

Degla knew the purpose of their visit to this forsaken place and awaited his master's sorcery to begin.

Vandermortel moved close to the edge of the uneven platform. The mammoth egrath's body, serving him well, had doubled in size several times over and now stood as a gigantic figure hugging the landscape and looking out through to the infertile land beyond.

Vandermortel turned and ripped a large branch from a dead and twisted tree, raised it high above his head; his other hand was raised in unison with the other. Bright lights transcended the length of the twisted stem, running up and down, churning round and around its core, the heat changing its very shape, turning it into a long, straight staff, now grasped and held gently in Vandermortel's grip.

Vandermortel turned once more and again faced the land beyond. This time his staff was held tightly in both hands. He waved the staff from side to side; a powerful force emanated from its tip like thick multi-coloured smoke that traversed the thin air, disappearing into the distance. A large resounding crack reverberated all around — then all fell silent.

Vandermortel did not move, other than to release the staff from the grip of his left hand, moving it groundward with his right hand and leaving it standing upright with one end touching the ground and the other facing directly to the sky above.

Moments passed. The silence continued. Then a deep rumbling could be heard in the distance; the noise grew stronger and stronger. It was like a million wings flapping in unison, getting closer and closer to the spot where Vandermortel now stood.

In the remoteness of space, a dim reflective light could be seen. The shimmering light got closer and closer as the sound grew stronger and louder; then the large approaching mass, becoming brighter and brighter, was drawn into focus; the image became sharp and clear.

Hovering just in front of Vandermortel were a thousand peglasaurs — silver, shimmering, armoured wings, capable of withstanding a dragon's fiery breath; hideous reptile features, protruding, pointed beaks, long piercing tails with enormous muscly legs, barbed talons, razor-sharp claws at their ends.

These flying creatures were the epitome of hell in the sky, and they were at Vandermortel's command.

Vandermortel turned to Degla, jumped back onto his neck and they flew off closely followed by the peglasaurs, escorting their new master as he flew back towards the Land of Dragons and the battle for Verow which lay ahead.

Astrolis heard the great sound high above his head before turning to see this mighty army approach.

It flew directly over their position and headed off towards the eastern shore and Vandermortel's assembled army of dark riders. This was not a welcome sight.

Degla set his master down beside Solway and Jeerplah, and the hovering peglasaurs dropped down and blended in amongst the amassed crowds.

"Now we have a plan," announced Vandermortel, *"at first light we will take to the skies and defeat Astrolis and his feeble dragons."*

Astrolis and his three generals sat well into the night, discussing their strategy and contemplating the battle to come, only too aware that first light would see Vandermortel and his hideous army advance on their kingdom.

Vandermortel mounted Degla. Solway took his place astride a giant of a peglasaur. Jeerplah was instructed to make his way along the expansive shore line and take all but a thousand dark riders with him, clearing this land of all who inhabited it as he did so; the instruction from Vandermortel was to meet him on the south side of the lake, beyond the Land of Dragons at the boundary of Verow, where they would join up after his victory.

Jeerplah summoned the dark riders, and they marched on southward, leaving Vandermortel behind.

Jeerplah wasted no time in following his master's instructions. As he marched southward, every village in his way was destroyed, the inhabitants massacred and the villages left to burn in their wake. This land was cleansed.

Vandermortel's legions of men waited for the signal and when instructed, mounted an army of peglasaurs simultaneously, swords raised, bloodthirsty for action.

Astrolis had set his army of dragon masters out strategically. This would not be one single encounter.

Stealth and surprise needed to play their part if they were to halt Vandermortel's progress south.

Astrolis's troops took to the air; instructions clear and precise, they flew off in every direction, spreading and hiding themselves far and wide amongst the high rocky outcrops, jagged rock formations and out of sight from the advancing flying army.

This was not an inviting landscape. The mountain peaks cast dark shadows over the rock formations spiralling upward from the solid ground and great lake's surface far beneath.

Rocks were sculptured into many shapes and forms by fine sand swirling round in the constant wind, which was cold, chilling and blew in constantly from the north, gaining strength, growing stronger and stronger as it drove on relentlessly.

Vandermortel's presence was felt in this land, churning up the surface of the vast lake, causing its waves to crash violently against its shoreline, thundering against the rocks at its edge and ripping at its very heart and soul.

The sun had risen, not that you could tell; storms were brewing, forks of lightning lit up the sky momentarily before vanishing, leaving an eerie foreboding, shortly followed by deafening claps of thunder booming all around, vibrating and shaking the very essence of this land.

Vandermortel had no preconceived idea as to how this battle would develop. His one and only focus was on transcending this land of dragons as quickly as possible and meeting up with Jeerplah and his remaining army on the other side; this day was a mere inconvenience and distraction for him.

Already mounted, this formidable army of dark riders astride peglasaur beasts charged from the subterranean landscape on Vandermortel's command, following their lord and master into aerial battle.

Flying, soaring through the air, twisting, turning, acrobatic, full of power, direction, purpose, the peglasaurs engaged with their foes in mid-air.

At every turn, as they passed each and every rocky peak, a new wave of dragons would descend upon them, attacking from nowhere, everywhere, raging fires emitted from their breath, swords brandished from the dragon masters astride their trusted steeds' scaly bodies.

From where he waited, Kane could see Vandermortel's army advance. He was watching expectantly, hidden in a ravine high up in the atmosphere.

As Vandermortel approached Kane and his kinsmen, each of them as brothers, known to him from birth, in unison they swooped down from the skies, attacking Vandermortel from high above.

The battle raged on and on. Kane found himself in a direct battle with Solway. The pair chased, attacked, flew at each other, the blades of their swords slashing the air as they moved closer and closer towards one other in the aura.

Great sparks emanated from the place their swords struck each other's, again and again and again. A surge of fire was rained down upon Solway by Kane's dragon, but Solway's peglasaur wrapped its giant wings around its new master, deflecting the flames high up into the night sky.

The peglasaur got the better of the dragon, and swooping down, drove its mighty claws deep into the dragon's flesh, gripping it tight.

This mid-air battle was fierce, ferocious, intense and bloody, both raining down blows on the other. The dragon's fire, used again and again, was of no use here. The peglasaur repelled the great heat, and fire rained down upon the dragon, continuing to protect Solway.

The colossus of a peglasaur spun Kane and his dragon round and around, building up momentum until it released the pair and sent them twisting and turning, flying uncontrollably, battering them into the adjacent sheer rock face.

Fatally wounded, the pair fell towards the earth, picking up speed until they crashed to the ground far below.

Having lived together, fought together, as one they had now died together.

Next to face the might of this army was Trellis.

A dead forest of burnt and twisted wood covered the steep hillside and acted as a temporary hiding place for Trellis and his brave men.

Vandermortel, leading the charge, was on them in an instant even without them realising it.

Trellis gave the command, and it was his turn to defend this dragon land.

The battle was no less intense: Vandermortel, the mightiest opponent of all, slaying every dragon along with its dragon master who dared take up the fight.

Trellis's men fought a valiant battle, but their numbers dwindled and dwindled until there were but ten of them left. This would be Trellis's last stance.

With the last of his brave men assembled in formation, Trellis stood in front of the impressive flying army hovering high in the sky directly ahead of him. This time at its head, Degla and Vandermortel himself stood in their way.

Vandermortel raised his staff; the power unleashed from its very tip sent a shiver over the landscape, reverberating around the sharp mountain peaks.

Vandermortel conjured up an impressive swirling cyclone and unleashed its power and very essence in the direction of his enemies. The swirling wind lifted up Trellis and his men, sucking them deep within its vortex.

Spinning them, rotating them, round and around, it trapped them inside, unable to fight back, paralysed by the great force holding them in and sucking the very life out of them.

The storm headed twisting ever skyward, far out to space, churning, revolving, picking up speed as it catapulted the unwary souls deep into the darkness of time and gone forever.

Vandermortel sat defiantly looking out into space. He could feel his great power return with every foe he defeated.

His power was growing day by day, his influence on this landscape clearly noticeable. Indeed, every landscape within the universe had begun to wake up to his evil presence, his power emanating far and wide, stronger and stronger, damning morality and benevolence wherever it reached, resurrecting the unemotional, dark evil that was Vandermortel himself.

His body was effervescing, buzzing, smouldering with random sparks of static electricity, small beads of light jumping and dancing around the surface of his skin wherever it was exposed, taking its time to settle down. Vandermortel was in no hurry to let this feeling go.

The feeling of power, of control, of destiny circulating around him, was sending a clear and unambiguous message to those who would dare stand against him — Vandermortel: his force was strong and it was felt like a pungent dark blanket slowly proliferating across every land, smothering good, choking hope, waiting for it to surrender and bow at his feet.

Slate, the last of Astrolis's great generals, readied his troops.

They took to the skies and soared higher and higher into the darkness, way above the approaching army, circling round and around, floating, gliding on the hot thermal air conjured up by their dragon's breath.

On Slate's command the great dragons tore through the air, spiralling earthward, gathering speed and momentum as they descended, driving silently at pace through the thin air.

Vandermortel was startled. He hadn't expected or prepared for an attack from above. Instantaneously, great flames engulfed their enemy, many dark riders were incinerated in an instant, leaving their peglasaurs rider-less and without direction, flying off blindly into the distance, departing the battle and leaving it far behind.

Vandermortel quickly reacted to the situation and brought his troops back into formation, seizing the offensive and taking the battle directly to Slate and his men.

The engagement was fierce, brutal, violent and ferocious, neither side giving in; casualties continued to rise on both sides, and the mutilated, falling bodies of all concerned turned the watery grave far below crimson red, as blood gushed down upon it.

Slate withdrew momentarily from the action and soared once again skyward, climbing high above the encounter far beneath.

On command his mighty dragon turned for one final time; he banked steeply to his left and immediately entered a steep dive, descending vertically downward, towards Vandermortel.

The pair hurtled down, faster and faster, steadfast in their determination to make this last attack worthwhile.

As the gargantuan dragon collided with the colossal Degla, the shockwaves emanating from the collision paralysed the entire battlefield.

The vibrations emanating from the impact were felt far and wide and stunned the very movement of all within the vicinity.

Slate's dragon and Degla were entwined together, tumbling, hurtling towards the ground uncontrollably. Swords drawn, Vandermortel and Slate traded blows, the sound of steel on steel smashing together.

Vandermortel's sword glowed hot, its end turning from silver to powder blue, then to deep yellow and finally red, as its tip increased in heat and intensity. With one final mighty blow he swung his great sword round, slicing though the neck of Slate's dragon.

Degla released his grip from the mighty beast and freed it, sending it crashing uncontrollably to the ground, taking Slate with it on their final, fateful journey together. Degla pulled himself upward and soared towards the sky. Vandermortel once again emitted great power as they did so. Glowing, drawing in and sucking up the power of another foe vanquished.

This land was almost transcended. Vandermortel waited patiently, pausing expectantly, postponing his advancement, looking forward to Astrolis making an appearance.

Vandermortel's army advanced slowly, passing carefully over the unwelcoming terrain.

As the high rocky peaks grew in number, closer and closer together, sheer rockfaces dropping downward covered green leaved trees stretching far out into the ravines as though suspended in mid-air, clinging on by tentacles gripping the very cliff face, struggling to hold on tight enough or stop the trees from falling to the ground far below.

As Vandermortel's army progressed through this bewildering landscape and travelled into an open stretch of sky, Astrolis was waiting.

Vandermortel roared with laughter as he saw this insignificant figure, alone in front of him. The last memento of resistance stopping him from moving through this land and onwards, towards Garouvious and one step closer to freedom.

Vandermortel commanded the remainder of his army to attack. As they advanced, a flash of bright light emanated from a spot just in front of Astrolis. It was intense, illuminating, so bright it could not be looked at directly.

As the light faded away, Zeelandia's silhouette, still cocooned within a glass dome, stood directly in front of Astrolis.

Zeelandia's beautiful figure, grasping a small, gem-incrusted silver staff in her right hand, looked directly towards Vandermortel and the advancing army.

Peglasaur after peglasaur crashed into the transparent shield protecting Zeelandia, exploding on impact, falling away into a thousand pieces, turning to dust as they showered down on the rocks far below, like snow falling from the sky, leaving a light grey blanket on the earth's surface where they finally came to rest.

Zeelandia raised her hands high above her head and quietly spoke in ancient Arcadian. She recited the same phrase over and over again.

"Compasaa, netoro, hallwadro, tumbellie."

Small beads of light escaped from the tip of her staff and immediately grew in number, swirling round and round as though pulled, twisted, turned by some great rotational force.

They consumed Zeelandia and hid her from the outside world. Their numbers continued to grow, glowing brighter and brighter as though waiting to explode.

Then without warning, they broke free from the glass dome and danced as one, as though choreographed, waiting for some orchestrated music to begin and ready to join in, hovering, watching over Zeelandia and the dome.

The light show climaxed and exploded into a billion minute specks of light, each one taking its turn to evaporate into the night sky.

When all around had settled, standing in front of Zeelandia was Vonarx and her impressive band of deadly butterfly people.

They formed a protective guard round Zeelandia and Astrolis, ripping peglasaurs from the skies with their great pointed spears and hurtling them into the sheer rock faces all around.

Zeelandia turned to Astrolis. *"My friend, for you this battle is over — take what remains of your brave people and your impressive dragons and let Vandermortel pass.*

"There will be many more battles to come — take your people, go and prepare for the days that lie ahead."

Astrolis was defiant. He would fight to the death; he would not abandon the fight at this late stage, regardless of the odds stacked against him.

Zeelandia brought reason to her argument and persuaded Astrolis to retreat with his men. Astrolis spun his mighty dragon round and headed skyward and out of sight.

As quickly as she had arrived, Zeelandia disappeared once more, a fleeting mirage, a ghostly figure, nothing more than an inconvenience in Vandermortel's eyes — her glass dome filled with a smoky grey mist, and she was gone in an instant.

The shape and form of Vonarx and her exquisite beasts altered. They were consumed by billions of light particles showering down upon them from above.

Their work here was done, and they too disappeared into the great vastness of space and out of sight.

Vandermortel found himself unopposed and moved forward towards Garouvious.

Zeelandia's Final Teachings
Lesson 1 — Time with Flymoro

Zeelandia sat alone in the chamber, perplexed, frustrated, annoyed that she was not yet in a position to help more with the physical battle against Vandermortel and the dark side.

She recalled her encounter with Astrolis and hoped that he at least was safe.

Even Arcadia, so far away from the conflict taking place, could feel Vandermortel's power grow stronger and stronger, day by day.

Adelphi walked into the chamber and sat in the chair opposite Zeelandia. She clasped both of Zeelandia's hands in her own and looked lovingly in her daughter's direction.

Zeelandia was not able to avert her mother's gaze, and the pair momentarily looked into each other's eyes.

Adelphi spoke in a quiet yet direct manner. She was not one for wasting words:

"My dear Zeelandia, we must make haste with your final teachings. Time is fast running out. As you are aware, you will travel once more from this sacred place with Heathrodece, but

before you take that journey, you shall spend time with Flymoro.

"She is indeed the greatest white sorceress Arcadia has ever known and she will share with you many of her powers — well, as many as she can in the short time that is remaining.

"Take some rest now, my darling — you will need all of your strength to pass this day by."

Adelphi let go of Zeelandia's hands, arose from her chair, turned and walked through the open door to the chamber, disappearing out of sight along one of the many corridors circumventing this unique, spiritual place.

Zeelandia sat quietly for a moment, deep in thought, contemplating the teachings to come and internally fighting self-doubt and belief in her ability not only to take on, but to defeat Vandermortel once more.

A single white dove flew into the chamber and rested on the arm of the chair where Zeelandia sat.

The dove initially made no sound whatsoever, its pale blue eyes open wide, looking comfortingly in Zeelandia's direction, its head tilting thoughtfully from side to side.

The beautiful creature quietly flapped its wings and rose majestically into the air; hovering just above Zeelandia's head, it then spoke to her, *"Flymoro is waiting for you in her chamber; please, follow me."*

The dove manoeuvred towards the open door and flew through the opening, circling close to the ceiling in the corridor just beyond.

Zeelandia stood up, walked slowly forward and followed the dove into the passageway ahead.

These corridors were no longer as Zeelandia had previously remembered. The sun shone brightly through tiny gaps in the ceiling, thrusting beams of bright white light into the passageway below, the light dancing and skipping off the stony floor, bouncing between the mosaic-covered walls, a brightness reverberating all around, looking for, searching out the darkest crevice to fill and illuminate, whilst at the same time delivering a calm, peaceful resonance to the entire area.

Zeelandia followed the dove along many such corridors, taking her time to absorb the detailed images depicted by the rich tapestry of stories unfolding before her as she passed them by.

Her mind was racing; without picking out anything specific from the intricate mosaic walls, she saw the history of Arcadia unfolding before her.

As her journey continued, Zeelandia absorbed earlier conflicts with the dark side: not just Vandermortel, Jeerplah, Degla, Galphia, but instead great battles with former masters of the dark side, far greater, far stronger and far wiser than Vandermortel was, or ever could be.

These rulers of the dark side had been in existence long before Vandermortel's rise to power. All of them had been defeated by the might of Arcadia and its allies in years gone by — Zeelandia could now see that there was hope that this conflict would end well after all.

As Zeelandia continued her journey along the passageway, the dove led her to an antechamber — a tight, square, open space with corridors heading off in three different directions. Tall, thin openings cut from the thick stone walls allowed light from the outside to shine through. Minute particles of dust filled the air, swirling round looking for a place to settle, each one illuminated by the bright sunlight invading this once dark and gloomy space.

The white dove floated above Zeelandia's head as though thoughtfully contemplating a direction to choose and follow.

As Zeelandia entered this open space, the dove drifted to the right and settled on a direction to survey.

The ground beneath Zeelandia's feet changed from a dark grey, cold, lifeless pathway to one shining bright with a medley of colours encased within an opaque lacquer.

At first the path had no visible shape, form of pattern, but upon closer inspection it was like a river of ever-changing colour, its flow taking a clear direction.

Zeelandia looked up. The white dove had disappeared; she was on her own now, with only this pathway to guide her forward.

She moved forward, tentatively at first; openings appeared on each side of the corridor, heading blindly off into the distance beyond. Dark, desolate and uninviting.

As she passed them by and stared down each of the alleys in turn, every one of them had their own demons to share.

Spine chilling sounds resonating off the walls, fossilising terror within.

Dark spirits inhabited this space and they were not to be awoken without consequence.

Zeelandia stuck to the path forged by the vibrant colours sparkling below her feet. She moved swiftly and quietly forward. In no time at all, she reached another fork in the path; she now had one of two directions to choose from.

The path ahead was no longer clear, once again cold, dark slate sat indifferently beneath her feet; the guiding footpath had disappeared.

The air was still, silent; both corridors were dark and uninviting.

Zeelandia stared at both. She raised her right hand, and gently rotated her wrist, pointing her palm in the direction she had chosen.

Zeelandia again spoke quietly in ancient Arcadian, almost whispering, as though too frightened to awaken sleeping spirits beyond: *"Sliporo, playaraga, jugmentah, courtana, mirropo."*

A bright light shone from her open hand, briefly illuminating the dark passageway ahead.

The light flickered and danced, skipping, pirouetted; then, to a crescendo of light and sound, a gathering of tiny fireflies flowed from her open palm and flew high into the air in front of her, bringing light and warmth to the cold, dark space stretching out before her.

The fireflies pirouetted, twirled, skipped and swayed, swarming round and around, moving slowly, but advancing with ease through the tunnel.

The pathway meandered sharply to the right, and as Zeelandia approached the curve stretching out before her, a dark, caped figure emerged from the darkness, extinguishing the light emitted by her escorts and plunging the area into total darkness.

The figure lunged in Zeelandia's direction, thrusting a pointed dagger towards her.

These dark cave dwellers were zorbas. They frequented these caves, searching for and feasting on lost souls; they were the spies of the dark side whose sole purpose was to bring darkness to the ever-shining light of Arcadia.

Zeelandia was ready for this hideous beast: one eye to the left of his face, no other facial features other than a skinny, scrawny orifice of a mouth, spitting and foaming as it attacked, cloaked, hooded, hiding its repugnant figure from the world beyond.

Zeelandia instantaneously thrust both of her hands, fingers outstretched, in the creature's direction.

A flow of energy surged from her fingertips, picking up this pathetic living thing, levitating it above the ground. She spun it round and around, faster and faster before releasing it and thrusting it against the side of the cave, turning it to dust on impact with the stony wall.

It was not alone; as though being released one at a time by the rock face and the darkness, zorba after zorba appeared before Zeelandia, attacking her from every direction.

Zeelandia raised her hands high above her head, closed her eyes and began to spin round.

A white whirlwind enveloped her, forming a protective shield, guarding her from her attackers. She was able to walk on, protected and uninterrupted.

Zeelandia continued her journey, and as she followed the path round the sharp bend to the right, a bright light filled the passageway. She walked directly towards the light, leaving the zorbas to retreat into the darkness whence they had come.

They were no match for Zeelandia. There would be no easy souls to devour this day.

Zeelandia passed through the light. Waiting on the other side to meet her was Flymoro.

The room they now stood in was long and wide, bright and welcoming; Zeelandia could see many archways leading to separate courtyards beyond. Trees, plants, herbs, strange animals. The sound of water flowing, birds and insects.

Each one was different, brought here to this sacred place, and each in its own right offering an insight into the power and diversity of the universe.

Flymoro had learned over the years how to capture and harness this great power and use its capability wisely, a secret she was now about to share with Zeelandia.

Flymoro walked through a small opening. Zeelandia followed closely behind.

The room beyond had table after table laid out. There was no particular order or pattern to the arrangement: large glass counters on which bundles of papers were laid, each one rolled up and tied with a different coloured ribbon; each lay strewn as though discarded in no particular order, each one gathering dust. Clearly, they had not been disturbed in a long time.

Two wooden tables to the rear of the room were adorned with glass tubes, beakers, mortars and pestles, and an array of instruments the like of which Zeelandia had neither encountered nor indeed seen before.

Flymoro spoke gently, turning towards Zeelandia, at the same time beckoning her to follow her into yet another room.

"Zeelandia, there is much to show you and considerably more that you must learn. The knowledge and the power I have gained has taken me a lifetime to both gather and understand.

"To show you each and every potion, each and every spell, to share with you the great powers of nature would be an impossible task in the time we have allotted to us.

"Today we will join together in mind, body and spirit — we will become as one, and through this union, subconsciously you will absorb my teaching, my understanding, my knowledge and my gift. Please, follow me."

Flymoro, closely followed by Zeelandia, walked quietly into the adjacent room.

It was not unlike the Chamber of Destiny in many ways. It too was constructed of crystal, but unlike the chamber she had encountered before, the pale and subtle changes in colour that adorned the walls there were not evident here.

The walls were a very pale shade of pink; the pink glow remained but did change its tone very subtly from time to time. It was peaceful, quiet, a place that would make meditation easy even for the most restless of minds.

The pearl white floor, cool to the touch, had an area covered in rose petals: reds, yellows and bright oranges, crimsons and pinks, each colour infusing together, bringing a collective union of colour and clearly defining a segregated area on the floor's surface.

One of the walls had cascading down it a gentle waterfall, a trickle of clear, sparkling, pure spring water.

Each drop independently meandered down the vertical wall until it reached the bottom, where it evaporated on impact with the ground below, rising gently into the sky as a light mist before disappearing once and for all.

Unlike the chamber, there were no stalactites in this room; the ceiling was like the sky itself, light powder blue with tiny puffs of white cloud breaking up the vista.

The picture it painted travelled the entire length of this great chamber and beyond.

Flymoro took hold of Zeelandia's hand and led her to the edge of the gentle waterfall.

The small, slowly moving drops grew in size and moved faster and faster down the rock face, growing in number; before long, water was gushing over its surface and crashing to the ground below, each droplet exploding into thousands upon thousands of individual smaller droplets, thrust upward from the floor into the room, catapulted high and far away from the pearl white floor below. Exploding and fragmenting into smaller globules as they were smashed against the first solid surface they came into contact with after their release.

Zeelandia could feel the temperature in the room begin to rise. This rise in temperature caused the small molecules of water to evaporate and form a thick white mist, floating just above the bed of rose petals in the centre of the room.

Flymoro asked Zeelandia to kneel down; Zeelandia did not hesitate in following her instruction and quickly dropped to her knees beside Flymoro.

Flymoro turned around; both were kneeling face to face on the edge of the petal carpet looking directly towards one other.

Flymoro took hold of Zeelandia's hands and asked her to close her eyes.

"Zeelandia — you will soon feel a force pulling you sideways into the carpet of petals — do not fight the urge to fall. Let your body move as though you are as one with the forces of nature that will call upon your body."

A few seconds later, as already advised, Zeelandia could feel her body's uncontrollable urge to fall sideways to the ground; she did not fight it, she let nature take its course as instructed. She was still holding onto Flymoro's hands and she could feel Flymoro fall with her.

The sensation of falling did not stop. She heard Flymoro tell her to open her eyes — they continued to fall further. The carpet of petals had wrapped itself around them both, cocooning them, taking them on a mystical journey.

Zeelandia's mind moved from a quiet, tranquil state to one that was racing frantically.

Her body became entwined with that of Flymoro.

Their legs, arms, bodies were as one, turning, somersaulting, spinning round and around — Zeelandia then found her thoughts, her state of mind change; she was no longer thinking independently.

Flymoro had invaded that space; she was now reliving past memories known only to Flymoro. She saw books, scriptures, potions, insects, reptiles, liquids bubbling away, emitting brightly coloured plumes of smoke. Everything was a haze, blurry, yet crystal clear at the same time.

The spinning and tumbling continued on and on, faster and faster; then without warning, it stopped.

Zeelandia felt herself rising upwards. She was now swimming deep, inside a pool of crystal-clear water, her body floating effortlessly towards its surface far above her.

Zeelandia reached the top and pulled herself free from the water and sat on a deep green coloured stone at the water's edge — she was not wet, she was not out of breath, there was no gasping for air.

A few seconds later Flymoro appeared from the pool and sat beside her.

They were no longer in the chamber. A circle of green stone ran all the way around the circumference of the circular pool, right up to the water's edge.

A carpet of deep green grass lay where the white floor once was; the area was completely concealed from prying eyes by a thick forest of tall pine trees spreading out in every direction.

Flymoro took hold of Zeelandia's hand, and the pair rose to their feet.

They began to levitate above the ground, hovering for a split second before Zeelandia felt herself thrust into the dense vegetation, all that the forest had to offer.

Zeelandia found herself flying through the trees, not round or over them but directly through them.

She became as one with its animals, its flowers, its insects, birds, animals, reptiles, absorbing into her skin the very essence of life this place and its diverse inhabitants had to offer.

Taking on, absorbing their secrets, their strengths, understanding their weaknesses and how they interacted with one other; and with that she soaked up the power offered to her by the unity of these souls when they all come together as one.

Without warning and as quickly as this experience had begun, it was over. Zeelandia found herself being thrown free from the carpet of petals that had once again cocooned her. She felt herself being catapulted across the cold, white chamber floor.

She was all alone once more — there was no sign of Flymoro.

Zeelandia turned and looked up. She once again saw the white dove hovering above her. It once again spoke to her in the same gentle voice as before:

"You have all that Flymoro has to share. You must follow me and I will take you to Heathrodece, who waits for you in the Chamber of Destiny." The tiny bird flapped its wings and moved once again into the corridor beyond.

Zeelandia's Final Teachings
Lesson 2 — Time with Heathrodece

The place Zeelandia now stood was no longer a stranger to her; she had visited this Chamber of Destiny many times, and she knew quite clearly what would be required for her to make the sacred journey one last time and take on Heathrodece's final teachings.

The two glass chairs were positioned exactly as she had remembered, with the column of crystal rods, as always, lying between the two chairs, each one neatly stacked and waiting to be chosen.

Zeelandia sat patiently for quite some time in one of the chairs.

The air was still, but crisp and fresh; silence filled the room; not a breath of air could be felt.

Zeelandia could feel her breathing deepen; she looked down, and her chest was pulsating to the beat of her heart, faster and faster, thumping, pounding, as though ready to explode.

She took a deep breath and composed herself. She closed her eyes and reflected on the long journey she had been on so far and the knowledge she had acquired with each of her encounters.

This brought with it a feeling of calm, and with that a level of composure. It allowed her to take stock of everything around her and bring focus and perspective to her current situation.

When she looked up, a tall slim figure was standing in front of her.

In all her beauty, Heathrodece, with her long, straight, black hair flowing almost to her waist, gently falling, unbroken over her tightly fitting long white dress, fashioned just like all of the other great White Queens' dresses of Arcadia, encrusted with tiny row after row of uncut and unpolished clear diamonds running the entire circumference of her waist.

Identical to all the others, a perfectly fitting tiara gripped the crown of her head; this one had no gems or precious stones set into it.

A simple, plain, platinum band, engraved with Arcadian scripture talking of love and peace, with doves and flowers etched alongside the intricately carved wording.

Heathrodece had long painted fingernails, bright red in colour, with one single diamond-encrusted platinum ring on the third finger of her right hand, the only jewellery to adorn her.

Heathrodece did not speak, but calmly took up her rightful place and sat in the chair directly opposite Zeelandia.

There was no need for words or explanations this time. Both were well aware of the sequence of events to follow — the only question for Zeelandia was what form this last teaching would take.

Just as Zeelandia had become accustomed, each of them selected a crystal rod from the bundle that lay before them.

They each offered their chosen crystal rod to the other, closing their eyes in unison, with the rods once again gently touching.

A resounding crack reverberated within the chamber and in an instant both Heathrodece and Zeelandia were catapulted skyward, sucked through space and time. Drawn towards the very essence of the universe and all the stars that it held within it.

Zeelandia felt everything implode. She felt herself being carried along inside a black hole. She had lost sight of Heathrodece at that time; she was all alone, being sucked, pulled, dragged in every direction.

She could see solid ground in front of her. She looked to her right and Heathrodece was there beside her, holding out her hand, beckoning Zeelandia to take hold of it.

As Zeelandia placed her hand in that of Heathrodece, they both crashed into the ground; they didn't stop — they travelled on, burrowing deeper and deeper, far beneath the earth's surface.

Zeelandia saw a long narrow tube, the root of a tree in front of her; the root turned in her direction and opened wide. It sucked both Zeelandia and Heathrodece deep inside its cavernous tentacle.

Zeelandia felt herself being swallowed up by this writhing monster, drawing her further and further along the path the root had chosen her to follow.

Zeelandia became as one with the tree itself. She was swimming in a river of moisture, being sucked up by this giant green monster; every particle of liquid was being used to quench the thirst of this magnificent creation, flowing with purpose to every extremity of the tree itself. Until it too had been extinguished, its job done, the tree's thirst finally satisfied, at least for the time being.

Zeelandia felt herself being stretched and pulled in every direction. Her arms, her legs, her fingers and her toes lengthened, extended, pulled to the point of almost breaking, until she filled every last inch of the tree's root system — its branches, its leaves and its exuberant white blossom, magnificently displayed for the world to see and admire.

She was now the life blood, the soul, the pounding heartbeat of this tree itself.

She took on its lifeform. As the tree swayed in the gentle breeze, she felt herself move in unison with it.

The wind grew stronger and stronger, rocking the tree back and forth. Uncompromisingly, the tree bent and twisted, creaked and roared in pain, swayed back and forth, determined not to be beaten or broken by any wind, however strong.

Zeelandia felt its pain. She felt its strength, its determination, and she too moved and creaked and roared in pain. She had become tree.

She stood there, suspended, majestically, uncompromisingly soaking up the might, the strength, the power and the stature of this incredible feat of nature.

She breathed in, slowly and deeply, absorbing all of the great power that had been harnessed by this giant tree over many centuries.

Slowly, she felt herself shrinking, and her body returned to its normal state. Every part of her body back where it should be, she walked forward slowly, stepping out of the tree's bark, and found herself standing once again on solid ground in the middle of a deep forest surrounded by giant redwood trees.

The intricate root systems that burrowed and meandered far underground in search of life-giving water broke through the surface where she stood, spreading far and wide, covering the forest carpet; rugged, twisting, gnarled dry wood lay unobserved, invisible to those who passed. Taking its time to survey life above ground, acting as protectors to the submerged, subterranean landscape and all the secrets it held, which for now lay dormant far below her feet.

Zeelandia looked up towards the thick canopy of deep green leaves gently swaying high above her head.

Of them all, one leaf caught her eye, its green colour not as deep as all the others. It was shiny, shimmering in the little sunshine that struggled to peep through the dense canopy above.

Without warning, it broke free from its tether and dropped softly towards Zeelandia. As it grew close, it increased in size. Zeelandia was mesmerised by the object — she couldn't take her eyes off it, not even for one single second. Its gently swaying motion, as it fell to the ground, had her captivated, hypnotised. She was completely caught up in its hypnotic spell.

Zeelandia closed her eyes. She felt her body tilt gently backwards. Her feet were lifted off the ground, and she started to levitate just above the earth below.

The giant leaf soothingly wrapped itself around her, swallowing her up and sheltering her, caressing her in a blanket of its own being.

Her blanket and protector became transparent, and Zeelandia looked out towards the forest ahead.

The leaf, her leaf, shifted position and moved off at speed, changing colour once again; all was dark within the protective shield encasing her.

Suddenly, a bright light illuminated the space she inhabited; she was still moving, she could feel the motion, but all was still within the vessel that carried her forth.

Her carriage grew in size. It was now one large open room.

Pure white walls, no windows or doors; then without warning, the space was overrun by creatures from the forest.

Bears, wolves, wild boar, birds, fish, frogs, insects. Creatures from days of old and now extinct.

They ran, they flew and they swam round and around her.

Zeelandia became entwined with them. They became part of her; she became as one with them.

It became clear to Zeelandia that the forest was not about the trees alone. The very soul and essence of the forest lies in the hearts of its inhabitants and the dependency they have on one another to survive and prosper.

The room became dark once more. The moving sensation slowed down, then ceased completely.

Zeelandia opened her eyes to find herself back in the chamber, sitting on the chair with Heathrodece sitting opposite her.

Heathrodece stood up and bowed in Zeelandia's direction.

"My great queen, the forest holds many great powers, powers you now at least partially understand.

"If you must use them, use them wisely".

Zeelandia had barely time to reply. Heathrodece turned, gently pulled on her dress just above the knees to lift it just off the floor, and walked slowly through the door to the chamber and out of sight.

Zeelandia's Final Teachings
Lesson 3 — Time with Adelphi

Zeelandia had barely caught her breath when Adelphi walked into the chamber and sat beside her daughter for what was destined to be their last time together.

There was little left to teach Zeelandia now. Her great powers far outweighed that of her mother, but what remained was for Adelphi to impart a sense, a knowledge, an understanding of the history of Arcadia and to share with her daughter the hard-won battles of the past against the powers of evil, the truth about the dark side, about Vandermortel's place in that history and an understanding of the importance this quest, her quest, would have to all who opposed the rise of Vandermortel and the dark side.

Adelphi was well aware that time was not on their side and that they must make haste with this final teaching.

Adelphi turned to Zeelandia. *"When you walked along the great corridors of this sacred place earlier, you saw the immense, impressive tapestries adorning the walls.*

"Those tapestries hold the history of Arcadia within their intricately woven fabric.

"Today we shall become one with those very tapestries. You will share in this rich history and through those tapestries you shall understand what has passed.

"The future is yet to be written, my child, but every day, those tapestries, which live and breathe all of our yesterdays, all of our todays and all of our tomorrows, will continue to be written — for good or for bad.

"Let us hope that the story currently being written has the ending we hope and pray for."

Zeelandia did not reply. She continued to listen intently to her mother, who continued to speak of Vandermortel and his progress through Citronus and the Land of Dragons.

"Vandermortel has grown stronger, and will continue to grow stronger with every victory he has. He may remain captive within the Gateway Stone but be sure of one thing: his power is now felt far beyond his prison; his armies and allies are growing in number day by day.

"We no longer have only Vandermortel to contend with; just as he did with Degla, Jeerplah and Galphia, resurrecting them from their stony graves, he is, as we speak, calling on the evil spirits of his ancestors, the dead armies of his forefathers to fight alongside him as he approaches Garouvious and prepares for his battle with Trevelous.

"Trevelous has his spirits of the past to fight alongside him, but I fear this battle of the living dead on both sides will be far from easy."

They both walked out of the chamber, turned right and headed off at pace along the long, dark and meandering corridor.

The tone in the corridor had changed as though sensing the urgency in the air. As they headed towards the tapestry, they were surrounded by a hundred zorbas, all racing towards them. Neither Zeelandia nor Adelphi were in any mood to be messed with.

As though tightly choreographed, the pair repelled their attackers with ease.

Hands outstretched and moving as one, bolts of light were released and rained down on these pathetic, misguided lost souls, breaking them into a thousand pieces, turning their flesh and bones to dust, left falling gently to the ground as Zeelandia and Adelphi trampled on their ash and continued their journey without giving any significance to the occurrence.

As they moved further and further along the corridor, Zeelandia could see the darkness of the corridor lighten. She could now see the beginnings of the tapestry quite clearly.

A tall white archway with pale pink roses growing up its sides and over its top was the foremost feature to catch her eye and the primary object to be represented within this engaging work of art.

Adelphi took Zeelandia's hand and instructed her to run — she did, faster and faster; the tapestry grew closer and closer with every stride they took, then suddenly and without warning, both Zeelandia and Adelphi rose from the ground and found themselves held captive within the tapestry itself.

Zeelandia was standing underneath the archway with her mother by her side. She could smell the sweet fragrance of the roses climbing around and over the glistening white archway.

A gentle breeze caressed her body and sent a cold chill to the very heart of her soul.

They both stood there silently. Zeelandia was unsure of what they were waiting for, or indeed, what Adelphi had in store for her.

Adelphi moved forward and walked through the archway. Zeelandia could not see what lay beyond but followed closely behind her mother, moving faster, trying to keep up with her.

Adelphi glided across the ground with ease, her shimmering white gown rustling gently behind her as she progressed. Then suddenly, she stopped, turned around and gestured for Zeelandia to keep pace with her.

As Zeelandia approached Adelphi, Adelphi raised her hands above her head and spoke quietly in Arcadian. *"Hoodenti, glassimo, fremco, domalacaa, seepoanaa,"* she repeated the same phrase over and over again. Nothing happened. All was still. All was quiet.

Zeelandia looked past her mother and could see a stream just beyond where Adelphi stood, crystal clear, flowing gently, slowly, quietly making its way softly down the hillside that was now visible directly in front of them, moving on and on far into the distance, eventually leaving her view, rolling out of sight, stretching far into the remoteness of the landscape that lay way beyond.

The banks of the stream were covered with brightly coloured flowers where Zeelandia and Adelphi now stood. As Zeelandia's eyes followed the course of the stream, the bright colours quickly faded, replaced at first with dull, dreary colours, interspersed with the occasional clump of vivid bright reds and yellows, then no colour at all as the bank on either side became dark, desolate places — lifeless, cold and uninviting.

A motionless pool of deep blue water rested in front of them. They approached the edge of the pool. Adelphi knelt at the water's edge and again recited the same phrase over and

145

over again: *"Hoodenti, glassimo, fremco, domalacaa, seepoanaa"*. This time there was a reaction.

At first, a gentle ripple was cast across the pool from one side to the other, moving with ease, uninterrupted, until it crashed into the bank on the other side, its immediate response to send an even bigger ripple back in the opposite direction towards Adelphi and Zeelandia.

On reaching this shoreline beside mother and daughter, the same thing happened again; this time a bigger ripple moved back to the other side.

Time and time again the ripple cascaded from one side to the other, each time growing in size and intensity.

The ripple became a wave, then an even bigger wave and then, without warning, thundered against the pool side, broke free of the pool and engulfed both Zeelandia and Adelphi.

The swirling water pulled them back into the pool and drew them far into its depths, then, without any warning, the great power released them, leaving them to float upwards unhindered towards the water's surface far above their heads.

Before breaking free from the water's grasp, Zeelandia felt something move beneath her. Unwittingly, she found herself sitting astride a gigantic, scaly creature, Adelphi by her side.

As they approached the water's surface all became clear: their saviour was Nadclo.

The giant creature safely deposited them both once again on the banks of the stream and awaited his instructions.

Adelphi turned to Zeelandia. *"The history of Arcadia has one constant: the stream of truth which has flowed through this tapestry since the beginning of time. It will continue to flow and tell the story of life and of hope as long as there is opposition to the dark side.*

"Nadclo will help us navigate this stream as it changes shape and magnitude, becoming a long and winding river, each of its turns shedding a new light on the history of our past and with that the fortunes of those who participated at each and every junction in our history.

"I will share this journey with you, but this is not my story to tell.

"Each of the great White Queens you have sat with has played her part in defining the history of our world as it is today.

"Bridgewater, Inchinnan and Ballantine have all played their part in the richness of our history, and you will see where and why as we journey along the antiquity of time depicted within the tapestry that now holds us within it."

Zeelandia listened intently to her mother, who gestured for them both to climb upon the back of the great Nadclo, which they did, unopposed and without any great effort.

Nadclo, without instruction, set off, swimming with ease, gliding through the water without even a ripple to signal his movement through the tapestry and the stories it held within this great work of living art.

Adelphi continued with her narrative:

"I will speak of many kingdoms, some close to Arcadia, some an eternity away. Many millions of light years, both in the past and indeed in our future.

"Kingdoms where great battles have taken place, or simply places with relevance in relation to where we now stand and the predicament we now find ourselves in."

There was no need for Adelphi to continue talking. The tapestry of life took over; it was as though Zeelandia was now living through past times, an observer, one with no influence or voice to be heard — just a witness to a bygone age.

The very first stage in her journey saw Zeelandia move through a peaceful land, a land ruled by the great Emperor Democrase. This was the Pulovering Empire — strong, resolute, but robust and fair.

Democrase commanded the respect of the entire universe and ensured that peace and harmony was maintained.

Resolving and judging on disputes — his decisions were final, and under his stewardship harmony prevailed.

As Zeelandia negotiated the first bend in the river, she could see great battles ahead.

A dark lord, Safron, was staging an unprovoked and surprise attack on Democrase and his mighty empire.

The Pulovering Empire was defeated, and all but two of Democrase's children were executed along with his wife and more than half of his great army.

Standing beside Safron, Democrase's eldest son Gyptolese now stood, having betrayed his father, his family and indeed the whole Pulovering Empire. He now took his place as Safron's right hand man, standing side by side with the dark lord.

Zeelandia saw one of Democrase's daughters, Floreso, make good her escape with the help of a White Queen, Pluro, one Zeelandia had witnessed in Arcadia but not one she had spent time with when she was there.

The great dark army of Safron, having defeated the mighty Democrase, moved forward, wreaking death and destruction wherever resistance to the cause of the dark side was found.

Gyptolese became a treacherous dark lord in his own right.

All was not lost; as Zeelandia moved forward, she could see a bright white light in the distance — it was Pluro and Floreso — and alongside Floreso she had amassed impressive armies of her own.

Many battles ensued between brother and sister as the tapestry unfolded; there was no love lost between these two siblings now.

As Zeelandia continued her journey, the next stage in history unfolded before her.

Gyptolese had two sons. Ahenobarbus — his name was well chosen. It meant bronze beard in ancient dialect, and as he grew into a giant of a man, he did indeed sport an impressive beard, more ginger than bronze in colour but nonetheless equally impressive.

His giant frame and his skill as a swordsman and fighter quickly earned him notoriety — feared by many, and that fear was not without just cause.

Gyptolese had a second son, Appius — smaller in stature than Ahenobarbus, weak of body and equally weak of mind. On his tenth birthday he was led by Ahenobarbus deep into the forest and did not return.

Many stories told of his demise; myths abounded, stories spread far and wide, each one more gruesome than the previous one, but only Ahenobarbus knew the truth.

Zeelandia witnessed the whole episode as it unfolded before her, and even she had been sickened by the gratuitous events she had witnessed.

Floreso had two daughters and two sons. One daughter was named Germana, who unfortunately died in a tragic accident when she was three years old.

Zeelandia immediately recognised her second daughter, Ballantine, and her two sons, Bridgewater and Inchinnan; all three were council members she was well versed with.

Until that moment Zeelandia had not realised the part all three had played in the history of Arcadia or indeed their importance to it.

Floreso, under the guidance of Pluro after fleeing the great battle for Pulovering, had sought refuge many light years away on a small planet deep within the Arcadian galaxy. Zeelandia could see the barren landscape that covered this desolate land, but the plan to settle here was well thought out.

The dark side were only interested in looting and plundering lands and civilisations that had wealth, minerals or precious stones, or lands whose allegiance was to the Pulovering Empire. They had no interest in such a worthless, desolate place such as this.

This land was to become known as Arcadia and it proved a perfect sanctuary for good to grow and for the forces against evil to regroup and form alliances for the future battles that would lie ahead.

Gyptolese's descendants grew darker and darker with each generation, the next generation more evil than the generation before.

Ahenobarbus had one son, Atilus, who in turn had one son of his own — Calvus, a ruthless barbarian. Powerful, but hunched over ever so slightly with a twisted spine. Unable to stand upright, bald, scarred and fearless.

Vandermortel was the current living descendant of this dark lineage.

Neither Inchinnan nor Bridgewater had any children. The line was continued with the birth of a baby girl to Ballantine; she was Flymoro, one of the great White Queens Zeelandia had recently spent time with.

Flymoro gave birth to a single daughter, Zeelandia's mother Adelphi.

As Zeelandia travelled through the centuries, the bloody battles, the victories and the losses on both sides played out before her very eyes, and the cost to both sides was clear for her to see.

Every battle left a scar, not just on the people of the time, but on the entire landscape of the universe.

As Zeelandia continued her journey along the river of truth, she witnessed every great battle that had ever occurred.

Those battles included the defeats of Degla, Jeerplah and Galphia and shone a light on the part each of the White Queens, including her mother, had played in protecting every corner of the universe from the rise of the dark side throughout the vastness of space and time.

Nadclo slowed down. There was one last bend left in the river to navigate, one last piece of the jigsaw to fill in, one story yet to be written.

The tapestry had already recorded Zeelandia's victory over Vandermortel, his imprisonment within the Gateway Stone and all that had passed to this very day — but the future was yet to be written.

Adelphi turned to her daughter, touched her gently on the side of her face with the back of her hand and faded away without saying a word, as though being written out of the unfolding story for ever.

Nadclo deposited Zeelandia on the far bank of the river. Beyond Zeelandia could see the opening to a cave. A white light shone from within.

A pathway rose beyond the cave, leading up to a small castle, square, squat with two turrets standing proud and upright, right on the water's edge, sitting perfectly positioned on the bank of the river.

The water was dark and still. Long shadows were cast over the motionless, silent river.

A perfect reflection of the castle and the surrounding trees on the hillside made it difficult to distinguish between what was real and what was a reflection.

The colours on the water were now changing and were as vivid as the colours of the actual objects they were reflecting.

The light grey stone formed the walls to the castle, interspersed with the dark grey lines, each highlighting where a perfectly placed stone would meet another, surrounded by the rich greens, browns, yellows and deep reds cast by the leaves on the trees, sharing with the world the forthcoming change in season from summer to autumn.

Zeelandia made her way along the edge of the river towards the entrance to the cave. The ground gently rustled as the newly fallen leaves softly cushioned her footsteps.

The light grew stronger and more intense as she approached the small opening, so bright nothing could be seen beyond the entrance itself.

Zeelandia stood in the doorway. The light intensified further. Zeelandia moved her hands above her head and spoke gently once again in her native Arcadian: *"Legooro, mitenalco, atamantah, fasceeto."*

A spiral of tiny stars gathered above her head, spinning round and around, faster and faster, growing all the time in number, multiplying over and over again.

Zeelandia dropped her hands down to her sides and the stars followed, encasing her in their own being.

Zeelandia moved forward into the cave; she moved slowly towards the bright light in front of her.

A door opened, and Zeelandia walked through. She found herself in a large chamber constructed solely from crystal.

She recognised the place immediately — it was the last place she had been before Ballantine helped her with her journey to the spirits of Arcadia.

The shimmering walls surrounded her, just like before; the colours flickered from white to pale blue, light pinks and glistening silver, ever changing, ever moving, mesmerising and captivating, drawing her closer and closer — it was just like waking from a dream; it was as though she had never been away.

"Welcome back, Zeelandia," a voice echoed in her ear. Ballantine was standing beside her, a hand outstretched, appreciative for her long-awaited return, safe and in one piece.

The two moved swiftly through the dark corridors and entered the large hexagonal shaped main chamber once more, where Kingston, her uncle, along with Inchinnan and Bridgewater, was waiting patiently.

Nothing had changed within the room since she left. It was as though time had stood still.

In fact, time within these walls had indeed stagnated, not moved on one single second; everyone continued to sit in

153

exactly the same place around the large intricately carved oval table, as before.

The intensity of the light had diminished considerably within this great hall since her last visit. It was no longer a beacon of light; the walls appeared to be devoid of any colour or depth, just as before, but this time, long grey shadows were cast heavy against what little light there was in the room. A sign of the times they now faced.

Zeelandia took up her place once again beside her uncle. This time there were no pleasantries exchanged or holding of hands. There was serious business to be discussed.

The Battle for Garouvious

This was no mortals' landscape; a translation of the word Garouvious was quite simple — it meant *"The Land of the Living Dead".* A description that suited it well for a number of reasons, and not all to do with the landscape itself.

This was a bleak, barren landscape, forged from centuries of volcanic eruptions. Much of this activity was long gone, leaving it silent and benign; but underneath, there remained signs everywhere of the ongoing, unstoppable volcanic activity that was still present, activity that continued to shape this hideous environment and its sadistic inhabitants.

The air was thick with choking black dust, picked up and thrown round and around by the sweltering, swirling winds, before being set free to fall as tiny particles, finally settling on the hard rock all around, lying as a blanket of pungent, decaying filth on the topography of this barren and apparently lifeless landscape.

Sporadically, plumes of molten lava spurted from the ground high into the air, having drilled upwards from far beneath this harsh environment, before breaking through its surface and showering the ground below as it fell.

Deep gorges forged by past activity snaked through the terrain as far as the eye could see, interrupted only by bubbling pools of hot liquid, sulphur rising into the atmosphere, sucking out the oxygen and replacing it with thick poisonous gases, making it almost impossible to breathe.

The air was so pungent it made your stomach churn in disgust. The putrid smell of decaying bodies thickened the night sky, or at least what could still be seen of it through the dark cloud that now cast a menacing shadow across this entire land.

Blackened trees and tree stumps were the only sign of past vegetation, long ago scorched beyond all recognition; these preserved fossils were the only hint of a land that was once the bearer of life in any form.

Great caverns rose from the landscape, forming a protective barrier to a land way beyond. Far away in the distance, a rich green valley could be seen, sitting quietly as though completely unaware of this godforsaken landscape that for centuries had acted as its guardian and protector.

Trevelous sat quietly on his own, high up on the mountainside on a narrow ledge. The ledge appeared to be unsupported and jutted out from the sheer rock face, which fell away vertically, crashing to the ground way below.

He was looking out over the landscape, his landscape, his kingdom, a kingdom that stretched out as far as the eye could see; he gathered his thoughts and contemplated the battle ahead.

He was soon accompanied by two of his oldest friends, generals in his mighty army, Hospicees and Maroco.

Hospicees had served alongside Trevelous's father, Treelie, and was at Treelie's side when he was slain in the great battle for Garouvious many years ago.

The battle was fierce and bloody. Vandermortel's father Calvus, on one of his bloody rampages, had stumbled upon Garouvious, and when he found it rich in precious stones and minerals, decided it would be his; he unleashed death and destruction upon it until it finally surrendered to his might.

However, Calvus's reign over Garouvious was to be short-lived, as within two decades Hospicees, with Maroco by his side, along with a young and revengeful Trevelous, took down the mighty Calvus, slaying him just as he had slain Treelie — leaving Trevelous to take up his place as the rightful heir of this land, with Hospicees and Maroco by his side.

Vandermortel hadn't been born at that time. He was still in the womb of Clavus's wife — Aglipta.

She had made good her escape during the short battle with a handful of the dark side's loyal servants, slipping away quietly in the dead of night, never to be heard of again.

Stories told of her death in childbirth, that Vandermortel was so big he tore her insides apart as he entered this world.

He entered this world covered in his mother's flesh and blood and with an ongoing taste for blood that could never be satisfied from that day on.

Trevelous knew this battle would open up many wounds and would raise the issue of old scores to settle on both sides. He was fully aware that the taking of his head would be high on Vandermortel's list of priorities.

He also knew that whilst Vandermortel was held prisoner within the Gateway Stone he was immortal — he could not be killed, just controlled at best, and even then, only if the

Gateway Stone were held safely once again within the vaults of Arcadia.

Not a battle that could be easily won. He had to stop Vandermortel or face impending death himself — a sacrifice he was more than ready to make.

Trevelous arose and hugged each of his comrades in turn — there was no need for words; they each knew that their destiny would be forged this very day.

They moved slowly down the steep hillside, one walking behind the other; waiting in the lush green valley below were thousands of Garouvions, his, Trevelous's people, standing side by side and alongside their magnificent white stallions, waiting for instruction.

The night grew dark; morning grew closer; Trevelous took his time and spoke to each and every one of his soldiers in turn. He walked amongst them until the sun rose low in the sky.

He climbed up and onto a rocky outcrop, where he turned and addressed his people:

"Soldiers of Garouvious, today we fight as one to protect our lands, our heritage and our future. Today we will succeed in stopping Vandermortel — we will stop him with the same courage and fighting spirit that saw us take back this land from his murderous father Calvus. We will show them no mercy, as they will show none to us. May the Lord and the might of Arcadia be with you all — today will be our day."

Swords were raised high into the air, thrust skyward in unison, seven times; each one met with a shuddering roar — *ARG -ARG- ARG -ARG -ARG -ARG -ARG!!!!!!!!* The sound resonated all around, deafening, threatening, confident, a bold display of their defiance and a true belief in their ability to fight for the survival of Garouvious.

Vandermortel was standing in the thick of the volcanic lands far to the east of Trevelous's position. There was no need for him to address his dark army — they were hungry for battle, hungry for death — happy to kill or be killed.

The dark riders astride their black horses, blades drawn, were menacing, imposing, and cast a dark shadow across this already blackened landscape.

Vandermortel had few words to say: *"Trevelous is mine. His head shall be placed upon my pole by me and me alone — do not touch him."*

His great army knew only too well why this score had to be settled by Vandermortel, and Vandermortel alone.

Dawn arrived and Trevelous's proud army set off in search of the battle ahead.

The lush green fields, the long grass swaying gently in the cool morning breeze, soon changed its form.

Before long they were moving over sharp, stony ground, the horses snorting heavily as they struggled to breathe in the choking blanket born out of the sulphur-enriched atmosphere.

Boiling pools of water failed to halt their advancement, each horse easily straddling any obstacle, whether liquid or solid, standing in their way.

The beautiful white stallions, galloping forward into this black landscape, looked mystical, like gigantic frothing waves rising up and breaking as they reached dry land.

Wave after wave crashed against the rocks and boulders, the jagged stone jutting out from the pillars of lava reaching high, skyward, swallowed up as though they didn't exist, as this mighty army advanced.

The great army progressed, moving faster and faster, their stallions eating up the ground before them as they closed in on Vandermortel's position.

Solway raised a large bone horn towards his mouth and sounded the attack. The dark riders were almost invisible as the cloths they adorned camouflaged them perfectly against the blackness of the world surrounding them. The vast army moved at speed towards the swell of the white tide that fast approached them.

The two armies engaged, swords cutting through the air, along with anything else in their way. Casualties heavy on both sides. Dark riders falling brutally to the ground, the same fate perpetrated upon the advancing army of Trevelous.

Trevelous cut his way through the hordes of dark riders, each one offering no resistance, no intent on their part to cut him down. They did not show the same mercy to Trevelous's men who died valiantly defending their land.

Each side inflicted crippling devastation upon the other until there were but a few left standing on each side.

Solway, using the same bone horn, sounded the retreat and called what remained of his great army back to his position.

Trevelous, along with Hospicees and Maroco, stood there defiantly; all but a handful of their brave army had been slain during this brutal encounter.

Trevelous knew what had to be done now — he sent what remained of his great army back to the grasslands, including his two dear friends Hospicees and Maroco, and set off at pace, heading to the base of the most active volcano in the land of Garouvious, Mount Galcark.

As he arrived at his destination, Trevelous dismounted from his horse and walked slowly towards a small opening in the side of the mountain.

What he was about to attempt had never been attempted or indeed called upon by him or any of his ancestors that had passed before, but both his fate and the fate of Garouvious and truly the fate of all Arcadia and indeed the free world depended on him at this moment in time.

Molten lava spouted from the top of the crater, throwing igneous, red-hot, liquified rock far into the heavens.

The stench of death was stronger than ever before. Flames rose high into the air like plumes of red, blue and yellow feathers, flickering and dancing in the wind, lighting up the night sky before being extinguished and replaced by another swath of dancing inferno, each firestorm flaring up higher than the last, burning and scorching the putrid air all around.

Trevelous entered the small opening; inside, a steep set of stairs led far below, spiralling down into the heat and dust beyond.

Trevelous made his way gingerly down the turning, twisting staircase, looking over the edge and far into the abyss. He could see a river of molten lava flowing through the very heart of the mountain — that was his destination, the place he needed to reach.

Eerie sounds filled the chasm, haunting screams, deathly cries, ghostly figures emerging from the cracks in the sheer rock face, flying, twisting, turning, following him as he descended further into the soul of this treacherous mountain.

He had no fight with them, and they intended no harm to him.

Trevelous descended further and further, the heat intensifying with every step he took. His escorts, these demons, protectors of the mountain, journeyed with him every step of the way; they knew his purpose, his reason to be here and their presence was a signal of their approval.

Trevelous could see his final destination. A few more steps and he would be there.

He stood silently on the bank of the molten river that now flowed past his feet.

The ghostly figures amassed in front of him, hovering above the river as though waiting for his instruction.

Trevelous raised his hands above his head and spoke in his native Garouvion — roughly translated he said:

"My greatest ancestors, I call upon you — the great spirits of the dead — to once again rise and help me in one final battle against the evil of the dark side." Trevelous moved forward and stepped into the river of molten lava — his body immediately consumed by the liquified rock.

As his body submerged into the swirling fluid, sparks, bolts of white light ricocheted from its surface, bouncing off the walls and each one wrapping itself round the ghostly figures still hovering in formation above the river.

When the light show ended, each of the ghostly figures themselves dived into the river as though in search of Trevelous, sacrificing themselves, giving themselves up to the smelted, igneous free-flowing hell running through the bottommost part of this mountain.

The deep crater became calm; the molten river stopped flowing; the heat diminished and its very being, its very essence changed — this once untouchable, misshapen boiling cauldron was transformed.

In its place, a dark, cool pool of water, still, lifeless, now filled the entire area. The air was fresh, still no sign of life in any shape or form.

Trevelous's white steed, standing motionless, waiting for his master to reappear from the narrow opening, sensed something had changed.

He became agitated; he began to paw at the ground with his front hoofs, left then right, again and again kicking up the black dust from the ground all around him.

The dust began to circle him, enveloping him, covering him and turning his coat from pure white to the darkest shade of black imaginable.

He reared up onto his back legs over and over again, breathing heavily, unsettled, excited, frantic; then without warning, he exploded into a hundred pieces — his flesh transformed into the shape of one hundred jet black ravens circling round and around, hovering just above the entrance to the mountain, drawn to the narrow opening in front of them.

In single file they flew through the narrow opening and sank slowly through the air to the cool, dark pool way below, hanging, suspended, floating just above the surface of the water.

They circled round and around, rising above the still water, gaining height, taking it in turn to swoop down and peck at the water's surface, causing a ripple to form and attempting to bring life to the lifeless pool.

The swooping stopped, and each of the birds perched on the rock face surrounding the deep waterway, as though transfixed, hypnotised by its very being.

Waiting full of anticipation, with trepidation, for events to unfold before them.

They were not to be disappointed — the water parted; the steps that had brought Trevelous to this very spot could be seen far below the surface of the water, now revealed as the water dissipated, continuing downwards and way out of sight into the blackness and towards whatever lay far beneath.

The silence was soon replaced by the sound of an army marching, armour clinking and creaking, swords and shields coming together.

Trevelous appeared at the top of the stairs standing on the step, level with the surface of the water; he moved on upwards through the spiralling staircase and exited the mountain.

He moved forward clear of the entrance and turned around.

Following closely behind was the great army of the dead: his ancestors, living corpses, mere skeletons; adorning shiny armour and yielding impressive swords, each had been summoned and each and every one had answered his call for help.

The black ravens flew out of the opening and circled round and around the macabre army as they awaited their instructions from Trevelous.

Trevelous said nothing. He raised his sword in the air, turned around and with his resurrected army behind him, charged into the night and in Vandermortel's direction.

Vandermortel knew what was coming, and now it was his turn to prepare.

Straddling a large black horse, he turned it round until it faced directly towards an imposing sheer rock face reaching high into the sky directly in front of him.

Vandermortel raised his long wooden staff high above his head, held tightly in both hands.

He swung his staff in the direction of the rocks in front of him and bellowed loudly: *"The spirits of darkness be with me, join me tonight and taste victory once more. I command your resurrection. I command your presence. Tonight, I deliver your souls from eternal hell to fight for me, to fight for the dark side and to defeat the feeble and weak presence that seeks to stand in our way. Join me once more and taste victory."*

The rocks began to shake and crumble. The ground began to open up. A long narrow trench appeared as the ground was torn apart in front of him.

A thick mist escaped from the opening, shielding the area from prying eyes. Then, without warning, rank after rank of hideous beings appeared.

No word could describe the grotesque, misshapen, monstrous and distorted beasts that emerged from this stony grave.

Ugly skeletons, some with flesh still hanging from their bodies, not quite decomposed. All shapes and sizes, creatures from throughout the universe, who had served and died for the dark side in battles long ago. Resurrected for one final battle.

Both sides charged towards one another, whilst Trevelous led his resurrected army; Vandermortel remained in position along with Solway and his other companions, Degla and Jeerplah, as they watched their repugnant army advance.

The engagement was brutal, but still Trevelous was untouched, no sword raised against him. Both armies fought to the end until not one single spirit remained standing on either side.

Trevelous stood directly in front of Vandermortel, Solway, Degla and Jeerplah.

Vandermortel instructed his loyal servants to remain where they were; it was his time to finish this battle and to seek revenge for the death of his father — he, and he alone, would have Trevelous's head as a prize.

Vandermortel dismounted from his horse, drew his imposing sword from its sheath and moved towards Trevelous.

"Today I shall revenge my father Calvus and advance to Mount Fleming unopposed — two prizes in one," he laughed long and loud. *"Where is the mighty Zeelandia — feeble like all the spent White Queens of the past, weak and pathetic just like the mighty lords who thought they were a match for me. You, my friend, I shall have mercy on, your end will be quick, and when your two friends Hospicees and Maroco come looking for you, they will find your head on the end of my staff."*

Vandermortel moved forward, an imposing figure standing head and shoulders above Trevelous, the egrath's tall, muscular body serving him well. Trevelous stood his ground and took out his sword in preparation for the encounter.

The terrain was rocky but relatively flat. Large worn stones made for sure footing underneath. Sporadic stalagmites littered indiscriminately around, protruding from the ground, some reaching six or seven metres in height, jagged, sharp, pointed, each one looking in no other direction but skyward.

The two swords came together violently, each combatant taking it in turn to wield his weapon and thrust it in the direction of his opponent.

Blow after blow rained down, sparks flying as metal met metal time and time again.

A heavy shield carried by Trevelous deflected many of the thunderous blows rained down upon him by his physically superior enemy.

Trevelous stumbled and fell to the ground, landing on his back; in doing so, he dropped his sword, rendering him helpless to fight back. Shuffling along the ground, moving slowly away from Vandermortel, the blows to his shield became more frequent, mightier, more ferocious as Vandermortel advanced, sensing his victory growing closer.

With one final mighty blow Vandermortel dislodged the shield from Trevelous's grasp, sending it flying through the air, leaving Trevelous unprotected, vulnerable and completely at Vandermortel's mercy.

Vandermortel moved closer to Trevelous and raised his sword high above his head, preparing to inflict the final fatal blow on his helpless foe.

As he did so, the whole area lit up; where there was only darkness light shone all around, so bright, so intense Vandermortel had to avert his eyes. When he refocused, Trevelous had gone. Standing in his place was Zeelandia.

Her breathtaking white dress flowed gently to the ground. Her long hair flowed neatly through the intricate tiara on her forehead. In her hand a long silver staff shone brightly and was pointed in Vandermortel's direction.

Vandermortel swung his sword with all his might in her direction. She lifted her staff and deflected the blow with ease. Blow after blow was rained down on her, each one tossed aside as though devoid of any power.

Vandermortel caught his breath, and in that very instant Zeelandia swung her staff in his direction and in one single movement cut though the egrath's neck, severing the Gateway Stone from the egrath's body.

Solway, Jeerplah and Degla rushed towards their master, but Zeelandia turned her staff towards them.

A large glass dome encased them, separating the oncoming trio from their master and Zeelandia, preventing them from progressing further. They could only stand and watch through their glass prison.

Zeelandia moved forward, preparing to kneel down and ready to pick up the Gateway Stone, and within it, its prisoner Vandermortel.

She looked into the stone and could see Vandermortel within; she said nothing. Zeelandia unwrapped a piece of delicately woven material, silver in colour, so thin, so light it blew gently in the light breeze now softly caressing this barren landscape.

Zeelandia placed the fabric on the ground and placed the Gateway Stone on top of it. She carefully wrapped it around the stone and tied it with a long piece of white silk ribbon.

Vandermortel and the Gateway Stone were now hidden from the outside world, and Vandermortel was once again held prisoner by Zeelandia and the might of Arcadia.

Zeelandia knew she could not pass through space and time directly back to Arcadia with the Gateway Stone from this land. It was too bleak, too desolate; the land still held captive and under the control of the dark side. Her powers were limited here, and dark, evil spirits still haunted this forbidding place.

Her only safe passage back to Arcadia was from the land of Henstridge, in the valley of Draghorn, a neighbouring kingdom where darkness had not permeated its tranquillity and beauty.

Zeelandia would not find rest until she had reached the sanctuary of that land which lay far to the east of the mountain range in front of her.

The Solomon Forest

Zeelandia picked up her trophy; holding it tightly, she embarked on her long walk up the steep mountain terrain that stretched out before her. This land was not friendly, and she would need to keep her wits about her if she were to transcend it safely.

The prison holding Solway, Degla and Jeerplah would not hold them indefinitely. It was but a temporary barrier, one that would vanish when the spell placed upon it by Zeelandia faded as she journeyed further from its location.

The narrow path snaked up and around the mountain's edge, barely wide enough to traverse in places.

The rocks underneath her feet were loose and slippery.

As Zeelandia made her way slowly up the pathway, the sheer drop falling away below grew greater with every footstep she took.

Barely into her journey, the rain started to fall, making every step up the almost vertical slope even more treacherous than the one before.

The rain grew in intensity, lightning forking down from the dark skies high above, striking against the side of the mountain towering above her location, dislodging rocks with every fresh strike, each one raining down on her from overhead.

The water started to run down the narrow path, flowing faster, getting deeper and deeper, now covering her feet as she walked on and on relentlessly upwards.

Before long, a small opening appeared in the mountainside, offering Zeelandia the opportunity to rest and shelter from the storm now raging fiercely around the mountainside.

Once through the opening, the space widened and revealed a concentric space, almost perfectly round with three separate tunnels leading off in different directions, each one fading away and out of sight into the darkness that permeated beyond.

Zeelandia placed the cloth covering the Gateway Stone on the ground and knelt beside it. She started to move her fingers as though playing a tune on some invisible instrument that had been laid out in front of her and only she could see.

She closed her eyes and spoke quietly in Arcadian. *"Morumenti, speradi, forentee."* She recited the phrase over and over again.

From her fingertips tiny fireflies were jettisoned, thousands upon thousands of them, swirling round, bringing light to the dark and cold space surrounding her.

The swarm of flies split in two, one swirling close to the ceiling high above her head, settling on a ridge running along the length of the hollow space she now inhabited, ensuring the room was light and bright.

The second swarm flew close to the ground, then settled on the floor beside her and turned themselves into a raging fire filling the empty, cold, damp space with heat and warmth.

Zeelandia sat contemplating the journey ahead, for the time being at least safe and protected from the raging elements encircling the mountain outside.

The night passed, as did the storm. Zeelandia stood up and walked towards the opening, assessing the journey that remained ahead of her.

The air was light, the sun shining down bright and warm, no sign of the violent storm that had passed, along with the hours of darkness.

She turned around and walked towards the Gateway Stone.

The ground began to shake violently beneath her feet. She could barely stand up. She reached to the cave wall, leant against it and used it to steady herself.

The ground opened up wider and wider, flames appearing through the opening in the rock; a long, thin, igneous molten rock in the shape of a hand emerged from deep within the crater and picked up the cloth shrouding the Gateway Stone and with it the Gateway Stone itself.

It shook the cloth off. Vandermortel could be seen, smiling, staring at Zeelandia and without warning, the hand vanished into the flames, taking with it the Gateway Stone and Vandermortel.

Zeelandia had no option but to follow — she threw herself into the opening, into the flames and felt herself falling uncontrollably downward through the inside of the mountain.

On and on, deeper into its very heart, the flames growing hotter, burning, scorching, the blistering heat almost unbearable, intensifying further as she tumbled downwards.

Her descent slowed and she came to rest, lying on an iron grate.

Below the grate fires flared all around, flames reaching up and caressing, kissing the underneath of the iron grate she now stood on; suspended just above the flames, she looked around, trying to see the Gateway Stone and Vandermortel.

She was locked within some kind of underground dungeon. In the distance in front of her she could see a large wooden door with a small hole in it; the hole had iron bars running from top to bottom. She could see through the opening and beyond into a courtyard.

In the courtyard there stood the Gateway Stone, standing upright at the top of a tall body fashioned out of the lava from the volcanic activity surrounding this mountain. The dark pliable rock, body shaped, immense in stature, turned to face her.

She could see the Gateway Stone at its head and Vandermortel staring at her. Imprisoned, she could do nothing but look on.

The giant figure stood next to Solway, Jeerplah and Degla; it moved forward and towards Zeelandia.

Vandermortel looked through the gap in the door and once again smiled in Zeelandia's direction.

"You are no match for me, O great White Queen — you will rot in this prison hell whilst I make my final journey to Mount Fleming and regain my freedom.

"There is no one to help you now, and your powers are futile here."

The giant figure laughed loudly, turned and walked back towards his evil servants.

At the far end of the courtyard a wrought iron gate was raised, and Zeelandia saw the four figures disappear into a tunnel beyond, the gate closing swiftly behind them.

Zeelandia was alone but not without hope — if Vandermortel were to be stopped, only she and Insignia could stop him now.

She mustered up all of her strength and called upon the fires raging below her feet. She called to them again and again: *"Socorro, teasmal, dongala, froptah — Socorro, teasmal, dongala, froptah — Socorro, teasmal, dongala, froptah."*

The fires began to dance in unison — swirling round, rising up, spiralling through the open grate she was standing on.

Zeelandia held her palm open and a ball of fire gently settled upon it — she blew with all her might and the fireball crashed against the large wooden door holding her prisoner in this godforsaken place.

Fireball after fireball followed the same routine until the force was so strong, so intense — the door was blown from its hinges.

Zeelandia moved forward, through the doorway and into the courtyard beyond.

As she approached the iron gates protecting the tunnel Vandermortel had taken, her attention was drawn to a small hunched figure in the corner — it was a stone statue, one she recognised from ancient scriptures — a figure that guarded this hidden gateway to the Solomon Forest,— the last sacred ground Vandermortel would have to cross if he were to reach Mount Fleming in time for the coming of the four Storms of Destiny.

If she could not awaken the statue, she would have no right of passage through the labyrinth of tunnels ahead, and Insignia would have to face him alone.

173

Zeelandia knew what had to be done; she bowed her head in the direction of the statue and knelt before it.

She put her hand to the ground and grasped a handful of the dark dust that covered the ground she found herself kneeling upon.

Zeelandia put her hand to her mouth and swallowed a few of the dust particles — her head tilted backwards and she fell into an immediate trance, her head moving back and forth, side to side. Then her head started spinning uncontrollably round and around, pivoting on her neck as though completely detached from her body.

The motion stopped — she opened her eyes and gestured to gently blow in the direction of the statue.

As she let her breath out, gold dust floated across the short distance between her and the statue, finally settling on the figure.

The statue took on a new, rejuvenated form, turning from a bleak, plain, nondescript grey to solid gold itself — the required debt had been paid.

Zeelandia waited for a second; the hunched figure rose to its feet, stood upright, well as upright as its deformed body would allow, and pulled on a concealed lever that had previously been hidden from view by the inactive, sleeping statue shape.

The large iron gates groaned as they opened slowly, not fully, but just wide enough to let Zeelandia slip through, crashing immediately shut behind her as she entered the tunnel in pursuit of Vandermortel.

There was no time to be lost. Vandermortel's trail would not be easy to follow through this warren of tunnels, but on she sped, relentless in her quest to catch him.

Vandermortel could sense Zeelandia's presence and wasted no time in advancing towards his ultimate destination. He knew Insignia would be no match for him on her own, but with Zeelandia by her side, it would be an entirely different matter altogether.

Zeelandia proceeded through the passageway with caution. These tunnels were no friend of Arcadia. They were indeed no friend to anyone.

The deeper the tunnels burrowed, the darker they became until Zeelandia found herself in total darkness.

She could hear faint noises in the distance. Scratching, squeaking, scampering — the stench permeating the atmosphere in this place was stale and musty, thick and pungent, growing stronger, more repulsive with every breath she took.

Without warning, a large rodent-like creature flew out of the blackness. Springing forward, it leapt directly towards Zeelandia.

She moved quickly to the side. Although she was blinded by the darkness, her senses were strong — it missed her to the right; she raised her hand and lit up the tunnel ahead; four giant panwas stood before her.

Salivating, crouched ready to attack, ready to feast upon Zeelandia's flesh and bones — formidable opponents.

The light shining from Zeelandia's palm grew stronger, more intense, so bright, so blistering — the heat emanating from her palm grew hotter and hotter. The panwas were helpless, nowhere to hide, nowhere to flee to — these creatures of the dark and cold were rooted to the spot. They were shrivelled up by the heat, forced to curl up into balls to evade the blinding light, unable to fight back. Zeelandia turned them to dust where they lay.

Zeelandia moved forward once more. She had no time to waste.

A fork appeared in the passageway, and Zeelandia had a choice to make, right or left — this was easy; she remembered this part of the tunnel from the tapestry of life she had journeyed along with her mother Adelphi — past battles had been fought here, and she remembered vividly the detail on the map.

She had no hesitation in deciding on which route to take and which one would lead her towards the exit, Insignia and the Solomon Forest lying beyond.

She chose the path to the left — now she could sense she was closing in on Vandermortel, but he was still some way ahead.

The underground pathway fell silent, an eerier, indescribable silence permeated this space. This was not a good omen.

Zeelandia pressed on, moving forward, slowly, gingerly — with a degree of caution.

Zeelandia had once again been joined by her miniature army of fireflies, who, in unison, continued to keep illuminated the way ahead.

They circled with purpose just above her head, moving forward, then falling back, keeping Zeelandia in sight and the way ahead bright and clear.

The silence was broken by the sound of running water. The passageway took a sharp turn to the right; the sound grew louder and louder as Zeelandia followed the course of the passageway; just as she turned the corner, ahead in the distance she could see a barrage of water, engulfing the tunnel and rushing relentlessly towards her.

The resounding roar from this torrent of water grew louder and louder as it approached, picking up speed as it thundered towards her.

Zeelandia had little time to react. She had nowhere to go, nowhere to hide — she had no option but to stand firm, face this giant water monster head on. She braced herself for the impending colossal impact and closed her eyes, awaiting its arrival.

There was no impact. Nadclo had arrived and swallowed her up whole, stealing her away from the ferocious torrent of water that now rushed on through the network of tunnels.

The water continued to come, flowing on and on, aggressive, wild, merciless, engulfing the whole tunnel network in every direction.

Then, as quickly as it had arrived, the surge of water ended and receded. Nadclo had no means of escape — devoid of water, his dying body, unable to survive, was already weak.

Nadclo opened his giant mouth and allowed Zeelandia to walk free, unharmed — his final sacrifice, his final part to play in this world. He slipped away, peacefully and without uttering a sound.

Zeelandia stood momentarily by his side, a tear running down her cheek, saddened by the death of this magnificent servant to the powers of good, and a true friend to her.

She was truly thankful for his intervention and his protection, but his ultimate sacrifice made her even more resolute, more determined that his sacrifice and the sacrifices of all those who had perished in this conflict would not be in vain.

Zeelandia moved forward. The end of the tunnel was now in sight; a dull light, but still a light, was clear to see in the distance. She wasted no time in making her way directly towards that guiding light.

Insignia's forest, the Solomon Forest, was silent. It had long expected, and now with trepidation, awaited the arrival of Vandermortel.

Insignia had no generals, no warriors to call upon. Her people were peaceful, gentle creatures — at one with the forest.

This was their forest, the creatures and plants they shared it with, and had no quarrel with anyone.

Yes, they could fight; yes, they would defend their land and block the way ahead, but this was not their way.

Insignia moved amongst her people and spoke to them — they shared with the forest and its many inhabitants their love for what might be the last time. W—hat lay ahead, what would transpire this day — one day, only history would report back on.

Armed with only bows and arrows, hidden, protected, shielded by the forest of which they became as one with, their only defence.

They moved deep into the forest and hid from sight — no plan to follow, no strategy for war. If Insignia signalled, they would act, they would fight, and they would defend their forest.

Insignia knew exactly where Vandermortel would make his entrance, but she knew not when or how many he would bring with him.

The sacred tunnel leading to this place had not been passed in centuries. Insignia knew this was Vandermortel's only route to the Solomon Forest, but how he would navigate his way into it and through it was unclear to her.

For now, she waited — guarding its exit.

Before too long, Insignia's attention was drawn to the small opening, partially concealed by overgrown vegetation.

A large hand appeared and pulled back the foliage surrounding the egress and stripped it from its anchor, tossing it to the ground. Vandermortel exited the tunnel network. In front of him he could clearly see the Solomon Forest and beyond in the distance his ultimate destination — the Mountains of Dean and Mount Fleming itself.

Solway, Degla and Jeerplah still by his side, Vandermortel knew this final journey would be no easier than any that had passed before, especially if Zeelandia were still in pursuit.

He had no doubt he could deal with Insignia and her people of the forest — but Zeelandia, she would be a significant obstacle to overcome if she were to reappear at this place.

Vandermortel instructed Jeerplah to stand guard over the exit to the passageway and sent Degla high into the skies — a reconnaissance mission, *"Survey the landscape, report back with what you see — locate Insignia."* Degla immediately took to the air, soaring higher and higher until he vanished out of sight.

Insignia remained silent, hidden from view; so far Vandermortel had only Degla, Jeerplah and Solway by his side — no great armies following behind, no dark riders.

Perhaps the three other lords had in fact succeeded in destroying every last one of his hideous followers.

Vandermortel and Solway made their way to a secluded area sheltered from the forest by a steep granite rock. Solway stood guard. His master, standing upright in the centre of the clearing, raised his hands high above his head.

His body, fashioned out of the molten rock, looked burnt, charred, scorched and stiff, but it continued to serve its purpose well enough.

Vandermortel knelt on the ground and begun to hammer his fist into the hardened earth, time and time again, relentless, powerful blows raining down on the stony ground.

The earth began to tremble, shock waves penetrating deep below the surface and echoing far underground.

The granite rock encircling this spot began to shake; cracks appeared in its surface. A small opening appeared to the side of the rock. Then everything fell silent once more.

Vandermortel stood up and walked across to Solway. He knew they would need help if they were to successfully traverse the Solomon Forest and bypass Insignia, the ruler of this land.

Reinforcements were called and were now on their way.

The pair moved to the side; a long winding root system appeared from the small opening that had just been forged and thrust itself high into the air, wrapping itself round everything and anything in its way — choking the life out of all it touched or indeed came into contact with its suffocating grasp.

The thick root spread to the edge of the forest and wrapped itself around the trees at the forest's edge, providing a bridge between the opening and the forest beyond.

The forest sensed something was not as it should be, the balance of nature had been disturbed and the feeling permeating this place was not a good one.

Insignia continued to watch from afar.

The tall trees at the forest's edge stood stout and upright, calm, motionless and silent.

The mood began to change slowly; a light breeze rose from the forest floor and hugged each and every leaf open to view. They rustled gently in the soft caressing puff of air now surrounding this place.

The wind intensified. The branches swayed back and forth violently as though trying to shake free from some mystical force trying to hold them back, restrain them, stop them from expressing themselves.

The wind grew stronger and stronger, its force unimaginable, but still the trees would not be broken; they bent, they arched, they bowed, but they remained defiant.

The wind ceased. The forest became still. A sense of calm prevailed, a calm that is usually followed by some unexpected happening.

Insignia watched on, still hidden from view by her forest. This forest, her and her people's forest, was now under attack, and she needed to understand what she and her people were up against.

Vandermortel turned towards the opening. A chattering noise could be heard in the distance from far below the ground.

The noise grew louder, more raucous, piercing, confusing, menacing.

Then hundreds upon hundreds of repugnant creatures emerged from the opening, climbing with ease along the root that had emerged from the same small opening a short while earlier.

It saw these ugly creatures catapulted high up into the trees at the edge of the forest; there they settled to await instruction.

Long skinny bodies, thin angular jaw lines, crooked sharp teeth protruding through the lipless orifices that served as mouths. Bony flat noses, long narrow pointed fingers, three to each of their four limbs, more claw-like than hand-shaped with long tails designed to grip and strangle.

Vandermortel's last army had arrived. These warriors were well suited to this terrain and the final challenge standing in his way, and all that now stood between him and freedom was Insignia and her pathetic band of elves and fairies.

Degla returned, circled round once and dropped down beside his master. He had nothing to report; the great Solomon Forest was quiet, no sign of life in any form.

"Check again!" Vandermortel bellowed, *"Insignia is here, I can feel her presence — find her, bring her to me."*

Degla once again took to the skies.

Degla's report did not make Vandermortel feel any more at ease, as he knew only too well what this forest could conjure up at a moment's notice.

Vandermortel wasted no time — he signalled his intent, turned and moved quickly into the lush undergrowth at the edge of the forest.

It didn't take long for Insignia and her people to engage, picking off the hideous creatures from afar, one by one concealed in their forest, arrows trained on their enemy, shots fired, targets hit and destroyed.

Vandermortel's vast army of creatures fanned out, offering protection and ready to take on whatever this forest would throw at them.

Their numbers were growing and growing, overpowering Insignia's valiant people, who were no match for this ruthless army and were soon defeated.

Only Insignia remained. Having returned from the forest, she now watched Jeerplah from above. Zeelandia was aware of her presence.

Jeerplah remained in position ready to pounce when — if — Zeelandia emerged from the underground tunnel. He didn't have to wait long.

Zeelandia stood there silently at the egress to the mountain and stood face to face with the imposing Jeerplah, but she wasn't on her own.

There was no Nadclo, but she did have Insignia by her side. However, if they were to move forward and challenge Vandermortel between them, they would need to take care of this commanding figure first.

Zeelandia stared directly into Jeerplah's eyes; he tilted his great head to one side to improve his vision and stared directly back towards her and Insignia.

"You know I cannot let you pass, dear Zeelandia, or indeed you, Insignia — I have my master's orders to follow.

"We can stop this now, if you will both join our great quest.

"Vandermortel will soon be free of the Gateway Stone and for those standing by his side when he is set free, he will offer untold riches and immortality. All that oppose him will be crushed and will perish.

"You, Zeelandia, have great power, of that there is no doubt, and that power would be welcomed and well rewarded by Vandermortel. H—ave greatness and be well rewarded or perish where you now stand — the choice lies with you."

Zeelandia drew a small silver dagger that rested neatly in the tiara she wore and held it out in front of her. Insignia drew an arrow from a pouch on her back and loaded her bow. Jeerplah laughed loudly:

"What is your intention with those feeble weapons? Neither are long enough or sharp enough to cut through my skin. If that is the best you have to offer, this fight will be short."

Zeelandia smiled and taunted the great beast to make the first move. Jeerplah was unsure. Was she serious, what threat could these delicate creatures pose to him?

He took one step forward; gingerly, he moved sideways, circling Zeelandia. Zeelandia stood her ground. Insignia moved to the side.

Jeerplah snorted, liquid discharging from his snout, dripping to the ground. He pawed the land beneath him with his immense hoof and focused on Zeelandia.

He was no more than three metres away from where Zeelandia stood.

She remained motionless, fully focused on the mighty beast and his every movement — he charged, head bowed, looking to impale his victim on one of his long, pointed horns, but he was not quick or accurate enough.

Zeelandia spread her arms out to the side of her body and flapped them gently; she rose from the ground, the movement quickly taking her high above Jeerplah and away from the raging beast.

Jeerplah turned quickly. Insignia was close by, too close — she was not able to react like Zeelandia. He took his opportunity and drove one of his giant tusks into her small frame. He turned his huge head and tossed her to one side like a rag doll.

Zeelandia moved with lightning speed, her arms in front of her and holding tightly onto her small dagger with both hands. Falling towards the ground, stopping directly above Jeerplah, she thrust the tiny dagger into his enormous neck.

On impact the dagger grew in size. It opened like a telescope. Zeelandia drove it far into Jeerplah's body.

The giant creature was fatally wounded; the ground shook as he fell — his time on this land, any land, finally over for good.

Zeelandia approached Insignia, but she had passed her last breath — she too was gone.

Vandermortel moved through the undergrowth and soon entered the darkness of the forest itself.

Branches on the trees moving, his army high up in the canopy, many on the ground moving through the forest like a giant tidal wave sweeping through this green landscape.

Vandermortel advanced further and further into the forest so far unchallenged, unopposed, marching on and on towards his final destination.

He could sense Zeelandia. He knew she was closing in. He knew she would not give up, but his determination to move on was unwavering. So long the hunter, he was now being hunted down himself.

He could smell freedom. It was at last within his grasp.

Zeelandia moved away from the oversized corpse and focused her attention on the dense forest beyond.

She stood upright. She could feel the wind in her hair, the cool breeze swirling round her body, gusts of wind growing stronger and stronger.

The trees around swayed back and forth in tune with the wind, bowing, bending as the wind tried its best to break each and every one of them.

Zeelandia became transfixed, hypnotised. She became as one with her surroundings; she too swayed in the wind in time to the tune played by all the trees of the forest.

This was her forest now, her domain, if not in body, at least in her spirit, and the spirit of Insignia now permeated this entire landscape — she was everywhere, she saw everything. She called out to the spirits of this great land and awaited an answer.

The forest began to close in on Vandermortel and his army — tree roots broke through the damp surface vegetation, picking up Vandermortel's foot soldiers and tossing them like the insignificant beasts they were through the air, dragging them underground and out of sight and lost to the visible world above the surface.

Below the surface, giant maggots and beetles fed on the flesh that was torn, ripped from the bodies dragged beneath the floor covering this sacred land.

Large leaves acted as shields protecting their limbs from the marauding army, branches turning to clubs and beating down any hideous creature who dared to rest upon it.

Vandermortel's army swarmed around him, protecting their master from this forest, which was now completely caught up in, and bound by, the enchanted spell cast upon it by Zeelandia.

Insects emerged from every gap, every crack in the trunk of every tree; they grew larger and larger, swallowing up the evil that surrounded them and threatened their land.

Still Vandermortel's mighty army could not be cut down. As quickly as they were slain, more and more appeared like a tide flowing out over the granite rock, filling the canopy with an endless stream of bodies, covering the landscape, refusing to be beaten back.

Zeelandia turned her attention to the source of this army. She twisted round and focused all of her energy in the direction of the large hole in the side of the shiny grey rock which continued to spew these wretched creatures onto this glorious land.

She spoke in her native tongue, this time with urgency, with purpose, *"Desolo, candarolo, mirrono — fernarmi, quesheedo, tompellia."*

Her eyes glazed over, only the whites of her eyes visible; she closed them momentarily; when she opened them once more, they were the most compelling shade of iridescent blue. Her whole body levitated above the ground, her back arched. She started spinning round and around, faster and faster out of control.

The vortex created by the spinning motion pulled great rocks and stone from far beneath the earth's surface, propelled skyward, each one synchronised, knowing its part to play and the journey it would be required to take.

Zeelandia's body stopped rotating. She slowly returned to the ground and pointed her hand skyward.

As though conducting an orchestra, Zeelandia directed the cavalcade of boulders in the direction of the granite mound.

Each one crashed into the rock face with unparalleled ferocity, raising the structure to the ground, sealing the gaping hole and stemming the tide of these abominable creatures from within.

She could now turn her attention back to, and focus on, Vandermortel.

Vandermortel pushed on through the deep vegetation, the elements within the forest doing their utmost to halt his progress.

His massive rock-hard frame was sharp, jagged and unyielding; unadulterated power was moving through this landscape with ease as his long arms, acting as two coordinated machetes, sliced through everything standing in his way — wood, bark, plants — trees a metre thick sliced through with ease and left to topple over, crashing to the ground.

His progress was relentless, moving forward, moving towards his ultimate destination with purpose, fully aware that Zeelandia's full attention was now focused on him and him alone.

Zeelandia had one last card to play, one final opportunity to stop Vandermortel before he passed through the Solomon Forest, but her time was fast running out.

She listened carefully to her surroundings and entered silent dialogue with them, resolute in her focus, decisive with what needed to be done.

Her action would destroy this wonderful land and all of its inhabitants, but the message passed to her by all who held this place dear and called it home, supported the action she knew she must take.

Zeelandia picked up a handful of dry twigs. She placed them neatly on the ground in front of her, creating a small bundle, each one painstakingly interwoven and stacked skilfully with care and precision.

She knelt down in front of the shrine she had just created. She pulled a locket of hair from her head and placed it delicately on top of the twigs.

She rubbed the palms of her hands together, faster, with incredible force. The friction created produced a ball of fire that now sat carefully balanced between her two open palms, swirling round and round, but sitting perfectly still in one spot, waiting for the command to be released.

Zeelandia slowly pulled her palms apart. The ball of fire remained suspended above the wooden statue she had created; then, without further instruction, it engulfed the locket of hair and the pile of dry twigs below.

The flames flickered and danced to the sound of a silent tune played by Zeelandia and heard only by them.

The small dancing beads of light and heat: yellows, reds, blues and oranges, grew bigger and bigger and turned into a raging inferno.

Zeelandia stood up and commanded them to set forth into the night, to seek out their enemies and to show no mercy.

The flames rose high into the night sky, illuminating the heavens above. Upwards they soared, swirling round and around, igniting everything in their path.

They formed a gigantic fireball, circling above and driving through the forest at great speed.

The flames separated and headed off in different directions, each one with its own purpose, its own target to ignite and destroy.

Within seconds the entire circumference of this vast area was alight, the fire raging from all angles, scorching the earth and all in its path, whether friend or foe, showing no mercy, consuming all in its way and leaving a smouldering trail of death and destruction behind.

Vandermortel with Solway and Jeerplah could feel the intensity of the flames closing in. Time was running out, as were their options and their likelihood of escape.

They were encircled, trapped. The wind was picking up, blowing stronger and driving the wall of flame ever closer to their position.

With one monumental effort Degla grabbed both Vandermortel and Solway, each grasped within the grip of each of his great claws. Degla flapped his wings frantically, trying hard to force a down draught and initiate flight.

The flames were upon them, the piece of land they stood on the last remnants of the forest, the only part yet to be consumed by this mighty fire.

With all of his strength Degla made it; just as the last parcel of land was incinerated, he rose high into the sky, taking his master and Solway with him, rising high up to safety of the heavens above.

Plumes of smoke rose high into the air, the charred embers of this once sacred forest laid bare; nothing remained but a desolate, blackened place, devoid of life in any form. Baked dry, branded by the mighty force of nature that had swallowed it up, engulfed, sucked dry and now left it to die.

The great beast circled the burning embers far below and soared higher and higher into the sky. In the distance were the Mountains of Dean with one mountain towering above them all — Mount Fleming clearly visible.

Degla's great wings did not stop. They cut through the thin air with ease, taking his master ever closer to his final destination.

Mount Fleming

Mount Fleming approached, its summit too high for even this great flying beast to reach.

Degla hovered carefully above a small ridge way up on the mountainside; the track led to a stout wooden doorway — the one and only entrance to this sacred part of the mountain.

Degla released Solway and his master, Vandermortel; they fell clumsily but safely to the hard ground below.

This track was too narrow for Degla to land on, but his job was done. He would continue to circle this magnificent mountain, ensuring its protection from the skies.

Solway and Vandermortel moved along the pathway at pace and reached the thick oak door quickly. Solway placed his hand on the circular wrought iron handle in the middle of the door, turned it to the right and then kicked the door open.

Vandermortel and Solway moved through the doorway and into the large open chamber beyond, closing the door immediately behind them.

They knew they would not be alone for long, so, would have to make haste; it was imperative they remained undetected for as long as possible as they made their way through the innards of this unwelcoming, isolated and bleak place.

Within two hours, their one and only chance in a hundred years would appear, and it was essential for them to reach their final destination before then, if Vandermortel's quest for freedom were to be realised and succeed this night.

The large open chamber led to a steep stone staircase at its far end; they covered the ground quickly, moving swiftly across the chamber's floor, overcoming this first obstacle with ease.

At the top of the staircase another chamber awaited them, smaller than the last, circular in shape, with small elongated openings in the walls that let in the cool air from outside and allowed a chilling breeze to permeate the entire space.

The stone ceiling was engraved with intricate carvings, basic in nature, full of colour and vibrancy, and told a story of this mountain and its history, of its people, its inhabitants from years gone by and of the place this mountain held in the history of the universe.

It told of good and evil, past rulers and great sorcerers and White Queens of this land and those who had passed through it on their way to new lands.

Not as intricate as the tapestry of life that adorned the walls of Arcadia, but no less important as a record of time gone.

Vandermortel had no time to take in the essence or history of this place; tonight, he was intent on adding his own chapter to this mountain's history and writing a new beginning for himself and for the dark side. A new chapter that started tonight.

At the far end of this chamber Vandermortel's final destination lay in front of him. Only two huge doors carved from thick grey stone hanging from equally impressive iron hinges, three on either side, stood between him and his goal.

Each hinge was fastened by six dark cast iron rivets, each one driving through the stone, secured out of sight in the room that was so far concealed and as yet unreached.

In the middle of the door a circle of raised wooden carvings protruded out, half on one door and half on the other door.

When both doors were closed, they formed a perfect circle, standing proud, holding secret the combination to opening the intricate lock mechanism that held this imposing door tightly closed and impenetrable.

Solway held the combination to this lock in his mind. Each wooden block had to be hit with precision in the exact order expected. If the lock combination were cracked, the door would open.

One mistake and entry to this chamber would be impossible, and all of the effort and sacrifice that had gone before to reach this place would be in vain. One mistake and the lock would self-destruct and vanish before their very eyes.

Solway took out his dagger from its sheath, the same dagger he had used on Lazonby so long ago.

He carefully selected the first object in the sequence he wished to strike. A king's crown, twelve pointed peaks to its top, jutted out from the door. Only three of the peaks were to be struck. Solway turned his dagger round, gripping the blade tightly, so tightly it cut into his hand.

The blood dripped down onto the cold stone floor below; Solway struck the wooden carving with precision. As commanded, it withdrew from the puzzle and faded into the door itself.

As the crown disappeared, an eerie sound permeated the entire mountain, inside and out; in the distance the guardians of the mountain had been awoken and would soon appear in a bid to halt this unwelcomed intrusion.

Solway needed to act quickly. Vandermortel urged him on. The next object took the shape of a tall pine tree. Solway carefully tapped three times on the object, and just like the crown it immediately disappeared from view.

Footsteps could be heard in the distance: the sound of something, life forces advancing, getting closer and closer.

The sound of many feet running across the chamber below and towards the top of the stairs close to the landing Vandermortel and Solway now stood on. Closing in.

All fell silent. Then all around a presence could be felt. Hanging from the walls, standing on the landing, suspended from the ceiling, creatures, a life form never yet encountered, stared down at Vandermortel and Solway.

Solway continued to work his way through the combination of the puzzle. One after another, he succeeded in conquering the conundrum before him, until only three remained.

A large reptile appeared at the top of the stairs, directly in front of Vandermortel; it exploded into a million pieces, with a hundred smaller reptiles emerging from the open corpse. They advanced and signalled the attack; all the creatures in unison moved with pace towards Solway and Vandermortel.

Vandermortel raised his hands in front of him, bellowing at the top of his voice. He clapped his hands together, each time harder, with more force, the vibrations were felt across the entire room. Shock waves emitted from his hands pushed back his would-be attackers, holding them at bay behind some kind of invisible force field.

He turned to Solway, *"Be quick, my friend, as I cannot hold them back for long."*

The noise was deafening. The screams and roars let out by the protectors of this mountain were deathly; as they failed to advance — the increasing noise reverberated round and around — low resounding wailing, high pitched screams, anger and frustration rolled into one desperate sound.

Solway opened the great door. He ran through, pulling Vandermortel behind him.

The door immediately closed shut behind them as they entered this final chamber, leaving the guardians of this mountain helpless, stranded on the other side. The closed door would never be opened again.

Inside, this chamber was expansive, circular, just like the previous one.

The walls were grey and plain, as was the ceiling.

A bridge traversed from one side of the room to the other, and a small ledge at either side of the bridge was the only support in the room and the only solid ground on which to stand.

Spiralling down from the bridge was an empty black hole that ran to the centre of this sacred mountain. Bottomless, black and cold.

In line with, and at perfect right angles to the bridge, the walls had four long thin openings — one each to the north, south, east and west. In the middle of the ceiling the roof was open, and the clear night gave way to a carpet of bright stars filling the evening sky.

All was quiet, all was peaceful, all was calm.

In less than thirty minutes, that would change — the four Storms of Destiny would arrive and if Vandermortel's plan played out, he would once again be free.

Vandermortel knelt down beside his loyal servant and bowed his head. Solway withdrew his long shimmering sword from its covering and presented it to Vandermortel's head.

With one mighty blow the Gateway Stone was dislodged from the temporary body that had served its purpose. Solway picked up the stone and with a single kick sent Vandermortel's spent body over the edge, falling downwards into the bottomless abyss far below.

Solway walked to the middle of the bridge, the two halves separated by a wooden plinth spanning the two rails running from one end to the other.

Solway carefully placed the Gateway Stone on the plinth. He reached into his inside pocket and withdrew the container that housed the opaque liquid and Lazonby's heart, the small organ still beating.

The heart was removed from the vessel and placed beside the Gateway Stone and the vessel discarded.

Solway retreated from the bridge and waited. In less than five minutes the four Storms of Destiny would appear and Vandermortel would at last be free.

Solway waited patiently. Vandermortel said nothing.

Zeelandia watched as Jeerplah rescued Vandermortel. She knew that they were now safely locked within Mount Fleming and only a few minutes away from their ultimate prize.

She could not physically make the journey to Mount Fleming — there was no time; she had become resigned to the

196

fact that Vandermortel would now soon be free of the Gateway Stone that imprisoned him.

Zeelandia walked aimlessly through the charred forest floor, surveying the death and destruction she had delivered to this once sacred forest — and for what? Her resistance had been futile this time, despite all of her teachings, she had not been strong enough, wise enough or clever enough to take on the might of Vandermortel and his dark armies.

She felt something cold on her head, something wet; she looked up, and a few tiny spots of rain dropped from the sky.

She touched her forehead, and a tiny raindrop, still intact, sat on the end of her fingertip, glistening, shimmering, shining by the light of the moon.

Zeelandia carefully placed the insignificant droplet on a diminutive deep green-coloured leaf that lay on the charred forest floor in front of her, the only vegetation that had escaped the ravages of the raging fire.

The leaf's edges curled up as though encasing the tiny droplet, storing it, preparing to feast on it at a later date when no one was looking.

Zeelandia stared at the leaf. It grew and grew in size until it was bigger than her, lying in front of her, still curled up, still protecting whatever it now held captive within.

The leaf began to open slowly, gently, carefully. The edges peeped open, revealing a deep pool of crystal-clear water within.

Zeelandia without hesitation stepped into the reservoir and fully immersed herself, absorbing its tranquillity, its refreshing, revitalising, energising properties.

The leaf carefully closed itself around her, cocooning her in its very being. She lay there motionless, suspended beneath the surface of the water — stationary, lifeless, completely at ease.

Her mind began to wander. Her past flashed before her, the battles she had faced, the comrades who had fallen to Vandermortel's sword and those of his allies.

This wonderful forest and the monumental sacrifice it had made — and for what? Vandermortel would soon be free, and she was powerless to prevent it from happening.

Zeelandia found herself floating, moving forward; the water was rushing around her, dragging her on and on, propelling her ever onward.

Spinning, rotating, spiralling out of control. Then it stopped; she felt herself floating upwards, higher and higher; then there was no water at all.

She felt herself catapulted through the very essence of space and time itself; Adelphi her mother was now by her side, holding her hand, guiding her on.

Adelphi let go of her daughter's hand and cast her forth into the ether of space, leaving her to absorb the power of the stars, the power of the universe, sucking in the very essence of sovereignty, of strength, of resoluteness and of determination and of possibility.

The wind blew stronger and whistled around the top of the mountain. Torrential rain poured down from the blackened skies above as the great Storm of Destiny fast approached this once sacred and consecrated ground.

Solway stood patiently, bolts of lightning ricocheted all around and could be heard crashing into and ripping gaping holes in the side of the mountain stretching out below.

Great claps of thunder bellowed all around as the storm intensified. The concentration of power awakening the entire universe, calling them as witness to the monumental event unfolding before them.

At the allotted time, the storm synchronised into four perfectly choreographed epicentres of destruction.

Each one taking up its allotted place in formation; one to the north, one to the south, one to the east and the final standing to attention, awaiting its command to strike; sitting patiently to the west of this impressive, commanding mountain.

The time was right and, as the scriptures foretold, the four Storms of Destiny in unison rained down their mighty avalanches of light and power upon the mountain.

The lightning entered the room as commanded through the four narrow openings and concentrated their great power on the Gateway Stone and Lazonby's heart.

The heat intensified, the stone began to vibrate violently, the souls of the universe whose very being made up the Gateway Stone, started to fade and break away, diminish and weaken.

An unexpected bright light shone brightly through the open space above. A figure could be seen hovering, descending slowly into this mystical place.

It was Zeelandia. Transfixed, hypnotised, she descended slowly, still falling, suspended. She placed her body in the direct line of the incoming lightning, preventing all four storms from striking the Gateway Stone at the same time.

Only blocking one storm, if she could act as a shield for a few more seconds, the storm would pass and Vandermortel would remain a prisoner for at least another hundred years.

The ferocity of the storm grew, her body was writhing in pain, twisting uncontrollably, contorted, consumed by the power engulfing her very being, but still she hung on.

A loud crack emanated throughout the chamber, a fork of lightning so strong reached in from above. It picked Zeelandia up, spinning her round, her tortured body held aloft — millions of volts of electricity flowing through her tormented body, too much for even her to withstand.

Her body became limp. The lightning lifted her up, spun her around and released her from its grasp. Her lifeless body fell silently, far away, downwards into the abyss below.

The storm intensified further. The Gateway Stone once again began to crack further, and the souls of the universe were finally broken.

All fell dark and silent. Solway stood up from his crouched position to see his Lord and Master standing before him — FREE at last.

The Gateway Stone had fallen and with it the might of Arcadia was finally defeated. A resounding black blanket permeated from this place and news spread quickly across the entire universe, signalling a new chapter in its dark history.